AN UNEXPECTED LOVE

A PRIDE & PREJUDICE VARIATION

LILY BERNARD

Quills & Quartos
PUBLISHING

Edited by Mary McLaughlin and Beth Flintoft

Cover by Tugboat Design

ISBN 978-1-956613-31-5 (ebook) and 978-1-956613-32-2 (paperback)

For MGM, whose heart abides in mine

CONTENTS

Prologue

November 1812

Elizabeth Bennet Darcy stared out the carriage window as the morning sun slowly peeked over the horizon. Uncontrolled tears streamed down her face as she watched the grounds of Pemberley slowly disappear from view. Taylor, her maid and travelling companion, kept her face averted and made no mention of Elizabeth's tears. She could not have been surprised to see her mistress crying; it was something she had witnessed often in their past months in Derbyshire.

In this dim light, I can barely make out the trees and the lake. How I enjoyed sitting on the bench watching the ducks and swans. Now I am on my way to another house I have never seen and wherein I shall meet many more strangers. I must use this time at Heatherwood to decide what I wish to do with the rest of my life. Perhaps I should use the money Mr Darcy gave me to sail to North America in the spring or settle in a small village somewhere no one could know me, and I can start over.

How did I ever get to this place in my life? When they learn the truth, will my parents be disappointed by my failure to stay with my husband?

As they so often did, the events of the recent past twisted and turned in Elizabeth's mind. As always, she was astonished that the events back in Hertfordshire could have taken so dreadful a turn for her. Seven short months ago, she had been a carefree young woman who loved to read, dance, laugh, and take long walks. She had helped her father with the estate books, tried to teach her youngest sisters how to behave like proper young ladies, and listened to her mother endlessly fret about her daughters' need to marry, to avoid them all being left in the hedgerows when her father died.

It had happened the day after the assembly in Meryton—the gathering at which Elizabeth, enjoying herself as every other young lady at the dance was that evening, found herself being insulted by a man who had not deigned to even be introduced to her. She had laughed it off among her friends, but it could not be denied that his words had haunted her, had even robbed her of sleep that night. She had left the house early the next morning, determined to walk off her dismay despite the foreboding skies above her.

How did I allow this to happen to me? Could I have avoided the accident that forced me to marry a man who was a stranger?

But no, she had not been able to avoid it—not the accident nor the marriage to a man who, after their wedding, never tried to know her and scarcely even spoke to her. A man who treated her as a guest in what was supposed to be her new home and only looked at her to find fault. She did everything that was expected of her as the mistress of a grand estate, but her husband never so much as acknowledged any of her efforts.

Elizabeth glanced at her maid, who appeared to have fallen asleep. She pulled a fine lawn handkerchief embroidered with *ED* from her reticule and dabbed at her eyes with it.

I remember Mama's excitement when she told us that Netherfield Park was to be occupied at last. Jane was mortified by our mother's matchmaking schemes even before she ever met Mr Bingley. I can still see Mama rushing into the sitting room...

One

April 10, 1812

"Girls! Girls! I have the most exciting news!" Mrs Bennet hurried into the sitting room fanning herself vigorously with her lace handkerchief. Her five daughters were seated around the room, each occupying their time with various tasks: sewing, reading, remaking bonnets, and, in Mary's case, poring over Fordyce's sermons. "Remember last autumn, we all heard that Netherfield Park was let by a wealthy young gentleman?"

"Of course, he never arrived and left us with nothing to look forward to," Lydia replied.

"Yes, we remember, but what is your exciting news, Mama?" Jane asked.

"Lady Lucas just told me he is coming this week! His name is Mr Bingley, and the servants are opening the house even as we speak!"

Elizabeth watched with amusement as her sisters received this happy news with varying degrees of alacrity. Mary appeared disinterested in the announcement, while Lydia and Kitty eagerly began imagining the balls this 'Mr Bingley' must intend to host.

"I am sure he will fall in love with you, dear Jane," Mrs Bennet continued. "You cannot be so beautiful for nothing—you were meant to be the wife of a wealthy man! I pray he and his party will attend the assembly next week."

Jane smiled at their mother even as she attempted to reign in her matchmaking scheme. "Mama, even if they do attend the dance, we cannot predict what kind of people they are or who they might enjoy spending time with. Perhaps Mr Bingley has married since the autumn and that is why his arrival here was delayed."

"Indeed not!" Mrs Bennet's enthusiasm was irrepressible. "Your aunt Philips told me that Mr Bingley is unmarried...and has five thousand a year! Imagine! Five thousand. He will make you a fine husband, Jane. I am sure of it."

Some nights later, Elizabeth sat elbow to elbow between Jane and Lydia as Mrs Bennet crowed her sister's triumph from across the darkened carriage. She listened with some amusement as Jane did her best to temper her mother's delight in the evening.

"Jane, my dear girl, you have done very well for yourself, very well indeed. I think an early summer wedding would be just the thing."

"Mama, we only danced. I hardly know Mr Bingley, and he danced with many other ladies besides me."

"Nonsense! Mr Bingley asked you to dance twice, and he stayed near you for most of the night."

Lydia could not be satisfied by Jane having all of her mother's approval. "What about me, Mama? I danced every dance tonight and had the most wonderful time. Perhaps I will be the first of your daughters to be married even though I am the youngest!"

"Jane should marry first," Mrs Bennet decreed. "When she marries an affluent man, she can throw the rest of you into the paths of other wealthy men."

Elizabeth rolled her eyes at her mother's assuredness, though she hoped that it might come to pass. It had been a mostly diverting evening for them all, Elizabeth included. The regiment that had been quartered in Meryton since last autumn ensured that there were always young men enough to partner the ladies of the neighbourhood, and Elizabeth had formed particular friendships with two of the officers, Lieutenant Denny and Captain Carter. They were agreeable, indeed, although she harboured no romantic inclination towards either of them.

Agreeable, she thought, *unlike some others I encountered this evening!*

As if she had heard Elizabeth's thoughts, Mrs Bennet asked, "And what of Mr Bingley's friend? He stood like a statue, not dancing with anyone other than the ladies in his party! Mr Bingley is so charming, and yet that Mr Darcy fellow was arrogant and disagreeable!"

Kitty reminded their mother, "Lydia, Lizzy, and I were dancing when he was introduced to you, Jane, and Mary."

"Well, you did not miss anything in that quarter. I heard he has ten thousand a year, but even his wealth would not make it worth living with such a disagreeable man!"

Elizabeth remained silent and held her breath, waiting to hear one of her sisters mention Mr Darcy's insults of her at the dance. She had been seated for one set, feeling rather overcome by the heat of the room and by her sore feet from a fast reel the dance prior. Mr Bingley, no doubt intending to be gallant but speaking from a position within her earshot, had urged his friend to ask her to dance. Mr Darcy's response, she feared, would be forever burned into her memory.

"She is tolerable but not handsome enough to tempt me, and I am in no humour at present to give consequence to young ladies who are slighted by other men."

Slighted by other men? She shook her head in the shadows of the dark carriage. No, he had been the only man who had slighted her. She had done what she could to appear unaffected, rising and walking past him to her friends, where she laughed to them about the rude stranger. Nevertheless, she feared his humiliation of her would soon become common knowledge within her family and neighbourhood. No matter that she cared little for his good opinion—no woman liked to be an object of scorn among her friends and relations.

The next morning found Elizabeth awake and out of the house even earlier than usual for her morning ramble. She walked determinedly in the direction of Oakham Mount and hoped her favourite vista would help clear her mind of that rude man.

I will not let Mr Darcy, that arrogant, dreadful man, keep me awake another night! His behaviour did not reflect his status as a gentleman—he sounded more like one of the stable hands when they think no one from the house is listening.

Did he think my hearing is so poor I could not hear his insulting words? Did I look that unattractive last night?

Elizabeth was hardly vain about her appearance. She was not tall, and her hair—a mass of unruly curls that tended to slip and slide from any arrangement her maid put it in—was generally untidy, particularly after an evening of dancing. Jane was, without question, the most beautiful of the Bennet sisters as well as the one with the sweetest temper.

I, on the other hand, am well known for my stubbornness and quick temper. I know I should not care about the comments of a stranger whom I pray I never see again, but for some reason it bothered me enough to keep me up most of the night.

Elizabeth looked heavenward as the skies began to darken; she could hear the distant rumble of thunder and pulled her shawl more tightly around her. *I must rid my mind of that terrible man before I face my family at the breakfast table. My mother and sisters will speak of nothing but the goings-on at the dance for days on end! And my mother will probably be pressing Jane to decide what colour she would like for her wedding gown and what foods she should serve at the wedding breakfast.*

As she walked towards her home, she heard hoof beats and looked up to see a man riding a horse not far from her. When he spotted her, he turned his horse and rode towards her, seemingly intent on coming to speak to her.

Of all the people on earth, Mr Darcy is out riding this early, and it seems that he wishes to speak to me. Quite peculiar, as we were never introduced, and he said nothing to me last night. Although he is very tall and handsome, he is a very strange man.

Elizabeth gritted her teeth. *I am in no humour to speak to anyone this morning but especially not him!* Attempting to prevent the meeting, she changed direction to avoid him just as it began to rain. She did not look over her shoulder but believed she heard the sounds of Mr Darcy and his horse moving away from her.

Elizabeth hastened her steps amid increasingly

frequent sounds of thunder and several brilliant flashes of lightning, as beautiful as they were alarming. The cool spring rain soon soaked through the muslin of her morning dress, and she thought of the scolding she was sure to receive from her mother when she saw her.

With her mind fixed on getting back to Longbourn, she was shocked by the intrusion of Mr Darcy, who had dismounted into her path. "Madam, the storm is getting worse, and your clothes are wet. I fear for your health. Pray allow me to help you return to your home before you become ill."

She stopped walking and gave him a tight smile. "I thank you for your kind consideration, sir, but your assistance is unneeded. I am a very short distance from home." Elizabeth continued to walk.

How in the world does he think he can help me get home any sooner? Perhaps he has another horse for me hiding behind a tree? I cannot believe he is worried about my health. He certainly was not concerned with my feelings last night!

Darcy caught up with her easily, the rain, now falling harder, dripping from the brim of his hat. "Madam, I insist you allow me to help you. I cannot stand by and allow you to fall ill when I can do something to prevent it."

She did not respond, and when the rain began pelting them and the lightning seemed closer and more frequent, Elizabeth increased her pace.

Intent as she was on avoiding him, her attentions

were too much on escape and too little on the path beneath her feet. A moment later, her foot slipped in the mud, and after the briefest of moments spent trying to regain her footing, she fell.

Mr Darcy was by her side immediately. After being assured that nothing more than her pride had been injured, he helped her stand. Without speaking, he led her to his horse. "Really, sir, this is not necessary. I am perfectly capable of walking home on my own."

"You have already fallen once, and if you fall again, you could break your ankle or worse, and then where would you be? I must insist you allow me to assist you." When she looked down, he indicated she place her foot in his joined hands. He lifted her onto his horse and then mounted it and sat behind her.

Mr Darcy held her firmly to him, with one arm around her waist, as they slowly made their way in the direction she had been walking. "I do not wish to ride too quickly and have Apollo slip in the mud. The storm is coming closer and closer."

Elizabeth, mortified and angry to find herself relying on the man as she was, said nothing. She pointed in the direction they needed to go, and they rode in silence for several minutes.

He should not be holding me this way. Anyone who saw us like this, with my skirts muddy and my gown clinging to me, would think we had been engaged in some sort of illicit liaison.

Uneasily, Elizabeth imagined what would happen if

some gossiping neighbour did think something of the like. What if her reputation was called into question based on something as silly as falling during an imprudent walk in the rain?

Luckily, no one else is foolish enough to be out in this storm.

A bolt of lightning hit the ground a few feet in front of them and caused Mr Darcy's horse to rear up. Elizabeth uttered a short scream, truncated by the abrupt dislodging of both of the horse's passengers. Mr Darcy grasped Elizabeth more tightly as they flew through the air and, in her fear, Elizabeth clutched at his arms. They hit the ground with a thud and soon lay motionless in the muddy field.

The Bennet family was accustomed to Elizabeth joining them when they were already seated at the breakfast table and were not surprised by her absence. After the family had almost finished their meal, Mr Bennet expressed his concern. "Lizzy is later than usual this morning, and I do not like the thought of her out of doors during such a violent storm."

"You worry too much," said Mrs Bennet. "She is probably taking shelter under a tree and will be home as soon as the weather improves. Jane, I am so pleased Mr

Bingley took a liking to you! Two dances! I would not be surprised if there is a June wedding!"

Jane sighed. Her efforts to calm her mother's excitement about the handsome Mr Bingley had made no difference thus far. "Mama, we only danced. Mr Bingley is a very amiable gentleman, but I assure you, we did not come to an agreement on the night we were first introduced!"

The youngest Bennet sister asked, "Jane, did you see the satin on Miss Bingley's gown? I did not like that orange colour, but the material looked so soft! Mama, we should all have new gowns for the next dance!"

Mr Bennet looked up from reading the newspaper, "Lydia, there will be no talk of new gowns or anything else this morning. You seem to have finished eating, and I suggest you think of something useful to do since a walk to Meryton in this weather is out of the question."

Mrs Bennet, undeterred, informed her husband, "We must see all our daughters advantageously married as soon as may be, and it is not as though eligible young men of such good fortune arrive daily in these parts. Jane is almost three and twenty—she must marry soon. If not, when you leave us, we will all be cast out to live in poverty."

"Madam, I assure you I am in excellent health and plan to remain so for many years; therefore, you need not worry so much about my demise nor any urgency for our daughters to marry. Excuse me. I will be in my study if anyone needs me."

Mr Bennet sat behind his desk and turned in his chair to look out the window. He knew it was not like his daughter to be away this late, and the rain had let up some time ago. He decided that if she did not return in half an hour, he would go out and look for her.

He occupied himself by sorting through an unopened pile of mail, but when more time elapsed with no sign of his daughter, he sent one of the footmen with a note to Lucas Lodge asking Sir William and his eldest son to help him search. Another message was dispatched to the Long's home beseeching Mr Long and his son Fred to join in the search.

When the Longs and Lucases arrived and the men set out, Mr John Lucas asked, "Did Lizzy walk her usual route today towards Oakham Mount?"

"I do not know where she went, but that is as good a place as any to start."

The worst of the storm had moved away, but a light rain returned as the men began to search for Elizabeth. They formed a line walking ten feet apart and surveyed the tall grass around them for any sign of her. In the distance, they saw a horse standing under a tree and walked towards it. Before they reached the animal, Sir

William signalled to his friend that he had found something.

Mr Bennet approached him and saw Elizabeth and a strange gentleman together on the ground very close—too close—to one another. Elizabeth's skirts were disarrayed, muddied, and, in one spot he could see, torn. Mr Bennet frowned, feeling alarm and a most unfamiliar anger stir within him.

"What are they doing?" Young Mr Lucas gaped at the pair. "They appear to be asleep, but why would they be resting in a muddy field?" His father was quick to silence him.

Mr Bennet spoke quickly, hoping there was something of his daughter's reputation he might salvage. "Sir William, George, I thank you and your sons for your help. If you will kindly keep what we have found to yourselves, I would be very grateful."

"You have our word, sir," said Sir William with utmost gravity. "Are you certain there is nothing more we can do for you?"

"I will handle things from here." As the Lucases and Longs walked back towards their homes, Mr Bennet looked down out the scene before him and shook his head.

I would never have believed this of Lizzy. Lydia or Kitty, perhaps, but not my Lizzy. There must be more to this than what it seems but...it seems quite bad.

His mind returned to the men who were with him, and he cursed himself for having asked the most unrestrained gossips of the county to search with him. *There is nothing to be done for it now. No matter how they got here, they have been seen together in an intimate embrace and must marry.*

Walking slowly towards the couple, Mr Bennet poked the man in the ribs with his boot. "Unhand my daughter this instant, sir."

The gentleman moaned as he awoke and slowly realised where he was. He gasped when he saw the young woman beside him. His eyes met Mr Bennet's gaze then returned to Elizabeth.

Mr Bennet looked away from the dastard on the ground and knelt beside his daughter. "Lizzy? Lizzy, can you hear me?"

Elizabeth slowly blinked her eyes, and as she began to wake up, she recognised that she was very close to Mr Darcy. With panic quick to flutter in her breast, she pushed him away from her. "Sir, you must move away from me this instant!"

"I am injured or would already be on my feet," the man grumbled, as he attempted to pull himself into a more appropriate position.

"Papa, I assure you, this is not as it seems." When Elizabeth looked at her father's face, she knew her words of protest were in vain. She was confused and in pain, but she knew what her father believed he had witnessed. It appeared to her father that she had been engaged in some sort of illicit behaviour with Mr Darcy, and she would be forced to marry this man—a person to whom she had never spoken a word and who had insulted her less than twelve hours earlier without knowing anything about her.

Her father addressed him. "Who are you, and what have you to say for yourself?"

Mr Darcy grimaced as he slowly got to his feet. "Sir, I am Fitzwilliam Darcy of Pemberley in Derbyshire, and I am a guest of Mr Bingley's at Netherfield Park. I assure you there is a reasonable explanation for this."

Mr Bennet regarded him with an icy glare. "Pray tell me what it is then."

"I was out riding this morning when I saw this young lady walking in the rain, and when the storm worsened, I witnessed her falling in the mud. I came to her aid and placed her atop my horse to expedite her arrival to your home. My horse was frightened by some lightning, and we were thrown to the ground. I did as much as I could to take the brunt of the fall. I suppose that is why I am in so much pain."

By the time he finished speaking, Elizabeth had pulled herself into a seated position and was staring at her hands in her lap, frantically trying to erase this morning's event from her mind and come up with some reasonable cause to prevent her being forced to marry Mr Darcy.

"I am Mr Thomas Bennet, master of Longbourn, and this young lady is my daughter, Miss Elizabeth. I became worried when she did not return home before the storm started. My neighbours helped me find you. The Lucases, as well as several other neighbours, saw you lying in the grass with my daughter. Despite their assurances to keep what they witnessed to themselves, in a small village such as ours, malicious gossip is often the only exciting thing that happens. I do not doubt the story will be spread abroad before noon."

Mr Darcy hung his head, looking as dismayed by the prospect as Elizabeth herself was. "Sir, I am an honourable gentleman. If it is absolutely necessary, I will marry your daughter."

Elizabeth looked up and cried out, "Papa, no! Surely that is not necessary! Nothing happened between us— you must believe me. How can we marry when we have never spoken to each other? We know nothing about each other and certainly share no affection."

Mr Bennet sighed wearily. "Elizabeth, it matters not what I think. In the eyes of Sir William and Mr Long and everyone who hears the tale, your reputation has been ruined. There will be no further discussion of the matter. You must marry him. If you do not, your character will be ruined, and you will destroy any chance of your sisters finding decent husbands."

Elizabeth began to cry and shake her head but knew

any efforts to change his mind would be futile. "Will you help me stand? I feel quite dizzy and sore."

When Mr Darcy reached for her hand, she said, "Not you. My father."

He kept his hand extended, and Elizabeth knew as he helped her up that this strange man was soon to be her husband. She was furious at him. Why had he insisted on following her? He was solely responsible for putting her in this situation. In a low tone, she hissed, "You should have left me alone as I asked. Your unwanted intervention is the cause of this terrible misunderstanding."

In equally outraged tones, Mr Darcy said, "I am a gentleman and could never think of leaving a gentleman's daughter sitting in the mud as the storm worsened. I offered assistance to a woman in distress. You could have broken your ankle or worse. The storm was right on top of us, and I feared you being hit by a falling branch or by the lightning itself."

He turned and looked at Elizabeth's father. "Mr Bennet, I will call on you tomorrow morning to discuss this matter further."

"Very well, I will expect to see you then."

"You have my word, sir." Mr Darcy bowed and held his side as he walked slowly back to his horse. He mounted with some difficulty but was soon on his way. As she watched him ride away, Elizabeth began to weep.

"Now, now," Mr Bennet attempted to soothe her. "I daresay that Darcy fellow will make as good a husband as any. Your mother told us at breakfast that she has already learnt he is worth ten thousand a year and has a house in town and a large estate in Derbyshire."

And is rude and haughty and insulting. Does he have any good qualities? If so, they had not been in evidence the evening prior.

"Papa, you know I care nothing about those things." She walked with her father's arm supporting her until they reached Longbourn.

When they entered the house, he advised her, "Go directly to your room and change out of your muddy clothes. Breakfast will be brought to you on a tray. I will not say anything to your mother or sisters until after Mr Darcy's visit tomorrow. Shall I send for the apothecary?"

"That will not be necessary. After a cup of tea and some rest, I will be well—or as well as I can be given the circumstances." Her father kissed her forehead and then turned towards his study, leaving her to get herself to the solitude of her chambers.

Elizabeth stayed in her room for the remainder of the day.

How will I be able to face my family tomorrow? I have always reprimanded Lydia and Kitty for their inappropriate behaviour around men, and now it is I who am being forced to marry because of a perceived ruination. I am responsible for my own actions, and I will not allow my sisters to be ruined because of me.

Darcy returned to Netherfield and found his host in his study. "Bingley, I must depart for London tomorrow. I plan to return in about a week."

"Why the sudden need to leave?"

"My friend, you may as well know the reason. I am to marry Miss Elizabeth Bennet when I return. I must obtain a licence and have my solicitors prepare the marriage articles."

Bingley stared at him a moment. "Marry? Darcy, you have only just been introduced to the Bennet family. If I remember correctly, you refused to dance with her last night and insulted her within her hearing."

Darcy had given his position considerable thought— or as much thought as could have been had on the short ride back to Netherfield. It must be imagined as a love match to quiet the gossips. "I realise you heard me say some things at the assembly that did not reflect my true feelings. I knew from the first time I saw her that I wished to make her my wife. I saw her again this morning while I was out riding, and happily, her feelings reflect my own. I am seven and twenty, and it is time I took a wife and Pemberley had an heir."

Bingley was doubtful for a blessedly brief moment.

"If you are sure, well, I wish you and Miss Elizabeth every happiness!"

"Thank you. Pray say nothing to your sisters. It is important no one know about our marriage plans at present. I know I can trust you to tell no one my news."

"If you ask me not to say anything, I will not."

"And would you stand up with me at the wedding?"

"Of course. It would be my honour."

When he returned to his chambers, Darcy sat at the escritoire and contemplated who he should notify first about the upcoming changes in his life.

April 14, 1812
Netherfield Park, Hertfordshire

Mrs Reynolds,
I am soon to be married here in Hertfordshire. Pray
have the mistress's rooms readied for our arrival at
Pemberley. I expect we will be there by month's end.
I would ask you to limit this news to as few people
as possible.

F Darcy

April 14, 1812
Netherfield Park, Hertfordshire

My Lady,

I must ask you to help me fulfil my request. Please order some clothes for a young lady of my acquaintance and charge the Darcy account. Choose whatever is the latest in fashion for day dresses, dinner gowns, and night wear. The young woman is not as tall as Georgiana and is quite slim and full figured. Pray have the clothes delivered to Darcy House as soon as can be. I will be in town briefly and will pick them up then. I thank you for your help in this discreet matter and kindly ask you share my request with no one.

Your nephew,
F Darcy

Two

Early the following morning, Elizabeth entered her father's study and found him reading. "Papa, I beg you! Pray do not force me to marry a stranger."

"Lizzy I am very disappointed in you," Mr Bennet said. "Had I been alone when I found you, perhaps we could have kept it between us, but Sir William and George Long and their sons saw the two of you together in the grass, Mr Darcy lying beside you and very nearly embracing you!"

"Papa, you cannot for one minute think there was anything to it but a terrible misunderstanding," Elizabeth protested.

"Perhaps, as you say, it was an innocent accident, but to all appearances, you had been intimate with Mr Darcy. I may believe your innocence, but you can be assured that our neighbours will believe nothing less than the worst has occurred."

"How could they believe I would give myself to a man I saw for the first time at the assembly? We had never spoken a word! I may have nothing in common with him. You are condemning me to a life of unhappiness, and I am certain Mr Darcy feels the same."

"What I may believe transpired does not matter. The appearance of impropriety forces me to consider how yesterday's events will affect the future of all my daughters. These things always have a way of becoming known, and then we would all be disgraced. I will not discuss this with you any further. Pray leave me now."

"What if I were to go away until the neighbourhood gossip moved on to another scandal? I could go to my aunt and uncle in London or anywhere else you suggest."

"If you run away, it will be an admission of guilt. If you have nothing to hide, then you must stay here and face what lies before you. I am sorry, but you simply must marry him."

The decisiveness of his words silenced her while her heart pounded in her chest. She knew her father was acting as he should, but she had hoped, obviously in vain, that a night's reflection would lead to some other solution. She could not look at her father any longer and knew her words would not change his decision. She ran from his study and returned to her room to cry.

Later that morning, Darcy was greeted at the door of Longbourn by Mrs Hill. "May I take your coat and hat, sir?"

"No, I will not be here long."

"Very well. I will enquire if Mr Bennet is available to see you."

While waiting to be received, Darcy paced the entrance hall and could clearly hear Mrs Bennet's high-pitched voice through the closed door.

"Oh Jane, Mr Bingley is so handsome! You will have the most beautiful children."

Mrs Bennet was talking, loudly and unrestrainedly, about Bingley marrying her daughter in a few months. *Whatever is she going on and on about? Bingley danced with her daughter, and they shared a cup of punch...but hopes of marriage after only one meeting? That woman has no sense.*

He was unable to hear what he assumed was Jane Bennet's response. He scowled as he looked around the small manor house, observing the furnishings and décor; he found everything to be quite dated and worn. There was chipping paint on many door frames and tears in some of the wall coverings.

"My dear girl, he has five thousand a year. You will want for nothing! And when you and Mr Bingley are married, you can introduce your sisters to other wealthy men."

The woman who answered the door appeared to be well trained. Perhaps she should oversee supervising the behaviour of the younger Bennet sisters. Their mother has certainly failed at that responsibility. This family is intolerable.

His thoughts were interrupted when Mr Bennet

summoned him into his study. "Good morning, Mr Darcy. Please take a seat."

Darcy noted that Mr Bennet's library reflected the same neglect as the entrance hall. Books and papers haphazardly covered every flat surface. Several stacks of books looked to be on the verge of collapse.

"I would rather stand, if you do not mind. I shall not be here long."

"Thank you for arriving so promptly. I understand your uneasiness. This is an odd business to say the least, but standing will not help the matter."

Darcy was unmoved and remained on his feet.

Mr Bennet looked up at the man before him. "As a gentleman, you must understand that it is my responsibility to look after the welfare of my family. Perhaps this was not the most fortuitous of meetings, but once you get to know each other, I am certain you shall see that it was fate that brought you and Elizabeth together. My daughter is an extraordinary young woman— beautiful, intelligent, well read, and very caring. Any man would be very fortunate to have her as his bride."

Fortunate? How can this man, my future father, think I can ever be happy about this union? I heard the way Mrs Bennet was speaking about Bingley and Miss Bennet and the inappropriate behaviour of her younger sisters at the dance. Elizabeth is altogether the wrong woman for me to marry, but I was raised as a man of honour and will do what is expected of me.

"I plan to travel to town today and arrange for a

licence and for the marriage articles to be drawn up. I am anxious to leave for my estate in Derbyshire as soon as the ceremony is over. I hope Mrs Bennet shall not be too disappointed at the lack of a wedding breakfast."

"The idea of you and Elizabeth marrying is still very new to you," said Mr Bennet. "I can understand your reluctance to hold a celebration of a marriage neither you nor Elizabeth desires. It will be as you wish. When do you expect to return from London?"

"I shall write and let you know when to expect me."

Mr Bennet nodded. "Once you have returned, we will schedule the ceremony for the following day. No use putting off the inevitable. I think it best that only our closest relations and a small number of friends be in the church. The rumours of a scandal will only persist and increase if we exclude everyone from the ceremony."

Darcy refrained from rolling his eyes. "I agree with your reasoning, sir, however, my only guest will be Mr Bingley, whom I have asked to stand up with me. I also asked him not to mention the marriage to anyone for the time being."

"I wish you a safe journey and expect to see you again soon."

With nothing else to say, Darcy bowed and left the room. It did not take long for the sounds of his carriage leaving to reach the study.

When Darcy was gone, Mr Bennet rang for Hill and asked her to bring Elizabeth to him. Elizabeth was quick to present herself, and Mr Bennet saw, with some regret, evidence of tears on her face.

"Lizzy, Mr Darcy has just left here and is on his way to town. He plans to obtain a licence allowing you to marry the day after he returns, with only our closest family and friends in the church."

"I pray he sees reason and stays in London and I never have to see him again!"

Mr Bennet gave her a wry smile. "If your prayers are answered, you will ruin your own and your sisters' chances of marrying well, and I cannot allow that to happen."

"I would have expected that we could trust Sir William and Mr Long to keep this quiet."

"It may be unfair, but you must marry Mr Darcy. One person forgetting their promise to keep quiet and everyone in Meryton will know what happened. Now it is time we tell your mother and sisters the news."

Elizabeth walked ahead of him silently as they went into the sitting room where Mrs Bennet and the other ladies were passing their afternoon. "Well, dear family, I have some very happy news to share with you. Lizzy is betrothed to none other than Mr Darcy of Derbyshire."

There was complete silence for a moment while they all reflected on his announcement. Then Mrs Bennet raised her arms in jubilation and cried out, "We are all saved! Ten thousand a year—he is as good as a lord! Think of the carriages, the gowns, and the jewels you will have! Oh, Lizzy, you have surprised us all! Now all my girls will have a chance to meet other wealthy men! How did you manage to catch the attention of a man like Mr Darcy—and so quickly?"

Ignoring his wife, Mr Bennet continued. "Next week, when Mr Darcy returns from London with the licence, they will marry and set off for his estate straightaway. Lizzy, start packing your things. Your mother will help you with the wedding arrangements."

Mrs Bennet protested immediately against these plans. "Why the need for the rush? There will be no time to travel to town to select her trousseau or plan the wedding breakfast. How are we to write and deliver the invitations in such a short time? How could you make plans for our daughter's wedding without consulting me? Have I no say in the matter?"

"I pray we are more fortunate with our other daughters and they will not have to marry with such haste. Lizzy, we must tell the family the truth or face a hundred questions a day." Elizabeth nodded, and Mr Bennet continued. "The wedding must take place as soon as possible to avoid gossip that might be problematic for the other girls."

"Oh, fie on gossip! What could anyone have to say of our dear girl?"

"They might say she was found lying in a field with him. And that would be the truth."

Mrs Bennet required but a moment to comprehend him. "Lizzy! Have I taught you nothing about behaving as a lady should? How could you do this to our family? Your sisters?"

"Mama, it is all the result of a terrible accident. I assure you my virtue is intact."

Mr Bennet added, "There is to be no wedding breakfast, as the newly married couple must leave for Derbyshire after the ceremony. If I ever hear of any of you telling anyone the truth of this marriage, you shall be locked in your rooms and have no pin money for a year! Have I made myself clear?" After a chorus of agreement around the room, he added, "Now, Mrs Bennet, I would like a cup of tea. This has been quite a morning."

After tea, Elizabeth trudged up the stairs and found Jane removing some of her sister's things from the wardrobe they shared. Jane held up a gown and said, "I thought you could wear this yellow dress for the wedding. It is in good condition, and you always look lovely in it."

"I feel I am being sent to prison with no chance of escape for a crime I did not commit."

"Do you have any affection at all for Mr Darcy?"

Elizabeth closed the door and sat on the bed. She told Jane everything that had occurred the previous morning. Tears formed again in her eyes as she lamented to her dear elder sister, "I want no harm to come to anyone in my family, but I still cannot believe what happened. I shall marry him to save you and my sisters from ruin."

She wiped her eyes and sighed. "I woke up yesterday and took my usual morning walk, and the storm came, and I was betrothed! How can I have any affection for a total stranger? I know nothing about him. Maybe he beats his servants and kicks his dogs. You and I have always said we would only marry someone we respect and admire—someone who touched our hearts. How can I be expected to respect and admire someone I do not know?"

Jane sat beside her sister and took her hands. "Unexpected love can grow between two people who never thought it could happen. You will have a long time to come to know and respect your husband. A life of mutual affection is not out of the question and is much better than many of the marriages we know."

Elizabeth scowled but Jane continued with her advice.

"Let go of your stubbornness and prejudices against him, Lizzy, and let your heart decide how to treat your husband. I feel confident you will find happiness with him. He must be an honourable man to marry you to save you and our family from ruin. You were not made for sadness. You were born to be happy. Feeling happy is a choice, and you must make the best of your situation."

The best? Elizabeth shuddered. "I feel doomed. I would run away, but I know Papa would find me and drag me back to the altar. I have no control over my future and that is what pains me most. Because of an accident, I will be married to a man to whom I have never been introduced."

The following day at breakfast, Mrs Bennet ordered, "Finish your meal quickly, Lizzy. We are for Meryton as quickly as possible. We must purchase as much of your trousseau as we can before Mr Darcy returns."

Elizabeth hung her head. "I shall be ready in a few minutes, Mama. I will take most of my things with me, so I do not need to purchase much."

"Nonsense! The wife of such a wealthy man must be dressed in only the latest fashions! Jane, you may come along as you have such a good eye." Elizabeth glanced at her father for support, but he refused to look up from his newspaper.

"How I wish I could tell all my friends about the wedding. We shall simply say that you are going on a trip with the Gardiners and require some new things."

Elizabeth was fitted for several new day dresses, a new bonnet, and a few other essentials while Mrs Bennet talked on and on to the shopkeepers about her second daughter's unexpected trip with her relatives. Shortly after they returned to Longbourn, their neighbours from Netherfield came to call.

"Mr Bingley, Miss Bingley, how lovely to see you both again. Please be seated. I shall call for tea."

Mr Bingley smiled broadly, his eyes lingering on Jane. "Thank you. We are very happy to see you all again." He turned his gaze on Elizabeth. "Miss Elizabeth, allow me to congratulate you."

"Why ever are you wishing Miss Eliza well?" Miss Bingley asked her brother.

Elizabeth explained as quickly as she could form her words, "I am to go on a wonderful trip with my aunt and uncle to the Lake District. We have just returned from Meryton where I began shopping for the new things I shall need while I am away."

Mr Bingley's face turned red, and he shot Elizabeth an apologetic look—evidently, he was in Mr Darcy's confidence. He said no more, but Elizabeth smiled, noticing he sat as close to Jane as possible.

"Are these the relatives who reside in Cheapside, near the docks?" asked Miss Bingley, her slight carefully hidden in her words.

Elizabeth ignored the intended insult. "Yes, my uncle is a very successful importer and has been generous enough to invite me to join them on their holiday."

"And when do you plan to depart?" Miss Bingley pressed.

"No firm date is set, although I believe it shall be within a fortnight."

"How will your family ever get over the loss of your enchanting company? Our dear friend Mr Darcy has gone back to town but he promised Charles to return soon. How we miss his fine companionship when he is away!"

Miss Bingley looked between Mrs Bennet and her eldest daughters, a cool expression settled on her face. "Have you heard of his home, Pemberley? Having been a frequent guest there, I can tell you it is one of the most beautiful estates in the county. How I long to return there this summer and spend some time with my dearest friend, Georgiana Darcy."

Mrs Bennet rose when the tea cart was brought in. "Miss Bingley, may I offer you a cup of tea?"

Yes, Miss Bingley, save your breath to cool your tea, Elizabeth thought, then rose to help her mother serve their guests.

The remainder of the visit went quickly. Mr Bingley rarely took his eyes from Jane's face, to his sister's clear displeasure.

One week after Darcy left Hertfordshire, one of his carriages arrived at Longbourn. Elizabeth was summoned to the servant's entrance, where Hill explained, "This young lady was asking for you, Miss Lizzy. She said she was sent by Mr Darcy. One of the footmen is bringing in her things as well as the packages she brought with her."

"I am Miss Elizabeth. How may I help you?"

The young woman curtseyed. "I am Anna Taylor. Mr Darcy has assigned me to be your new lady's maid, madam. I have brought you some new clothes. They are a gift from Miss Darcy."

Just then, Mrs Bennet came to see what the commotion was about, Elizabeth's sisters trailing behind her. "What is the reason for all this noise?"

"Mama, Mr Darcy has sent me my own maid and his sister has purchased some new clothes for me."

"Let me see those boxes!" After perusing a few of them, her mother looked up and declared, "Why, these are from the finest modistes on Bond Street. You must open them immediately."

"Pray allow Taylor and me to unpack them, and then I will be happy to show everything to you." Elizabeth gestured for the girl to follow her and then began to move towards the stair and her bedchamber as her sisters began to complain.

"Mama, why does Lizzy get all the nice things?" Lydia whined. "She has nearly disgraced the family and now she will have the best gowns London has to offer."

"Hush, Lydia. Once Lizzy is married, she will be able to arrange for all of you to meet equally wealthy men—perhaps even a member of the nobility!"

"Do you really think so?" Kitty asked excitedly.

"I predict that you will all be advantageously married—and sooner than you think!"

Elizabeth shook her head at their silly effusions. She entered the bedchamber and was amazed by the number of parcels which had been laid out. "What is all this?"

Sounding like she was giving some sort of recitation, Taylor said, "Miss Darcy, your future sister, is looking forward to meeting you and hopes you like what she chose. Mr Darcy told her you would not have enough time before the wedding to purchase your trousseau."

"I suppose we should begin opening them to see what needs alteration. The biggest package should be opened first." Elizabeth unwrapped the box and held up a beautiful rose-pink gown with a little gasp. It was very beautiful. "I can wear this one to the wedding."

"Oh, no. That is a dinner gown, miss. I can help you learn which dresses you should wear for different occasions."

Elizabeth sat down on her bed clutching the dress to her chest and sadly shook her head.

Taylor looked at her with concern. "What is all this fuss about, miss? No need to be upset. All brides are nervous before their weddings. I have worked at Pemberley and Darcy House for more than five years, and there is no finer master than Mr Darcy. He treats everyone fairly and with kindness."

I suppose I will have the loveliest dresses and shoes and everything else a woman of means requires after my marriage. I may feel like I have been sentenced to prison, but at least I will be well dressed!

"Taylor, let us begin unpacking everything and see how well they fit."

"Yes, miss, right away."

Darcy House was thankfully quiet—Darcy's sister was staying at Matlock House, and thus he did not see her or his cousin Fitzwilliam. The solitude allowed him to work quickly through the list of duties and obligations required for a hasty wedding. Within a few days of arriving in London, he obtained the special licence. Then he met with his solicitors about the marriage settlement, warning them not to speak of the wedding to anyone. He received the delivery of the new gowns his aunt had ordered for his intended bride, and sent them and her new lady's maid to Longbourn. When he finished his business for the day, he withdrew to his study where he drank heavily to keep from thinking about his future with someone so far beneath him.

April 21, 1812
Dearest Georgiana,

I have news which I am certain shall surprise you. I am to be married to a lovely young woman I met here in Hertfordshire. Her name is Elizabeth Bennet, and she is the daughter of a gentleman who owns an estate quite near to the one Bingley leased. She is lovely and charming, and I am certain you will quickly become the best of friends. Immediately after the ceremony we will travel to Pemberley, and you will meet your new sister when Richard escorts you there in the next fortnight. Pray say nothing about this matter to anyone until you and I have had an opportunity to speak in person.

Your loving brother,
Fitzwilliam

April 21, 1812
    Darcy House, London

Mr Bennet,
    I plan to travel to Hertfordshire on the morrow. I

*have obtained a licence and am prepared to marry your
daughter on the day after my return.*

F Darcy

Ten days after he arrived in London, he was travelling
back towards his ill-fated marriage.

Three

On the morning after Darcy arrived back in Hertfordshire, he and Bingley left Netherfield Park in two carriages—one to convey the newly married Mr and Mrs Darcy on their way north and the other to return Bingley to his house. The remainder of the estate's residents were still abed, and the two friends were able to leave without anyone awake to question where they were going.

Darcy could nearly feel Bingley's eyes upon him. Without turning his head from his study of the passing landscape, he said, "Thank you for your time this morning."

"I do not know what to say, old man—only that I hope it all works for the best."

"How could it? She and I have never even spoken to one another, and from what I have seen of the family..." Darcy barely restrained a shudder. "If she is anything like her mother, I do not know how I shall bear it."

"She is very well regarded in the neighbourhood."

Bingley's reassurances failed to console his friend; Darcy was too well invested in his own desolation. "I thought I was doing the right thing, and now I am condemned to live the rest of my life with a stranger."

43

"Even the dearest, most intimate friends begin as strangers," Bingley opined. "Although your marriage is unexpected, I can only hope your journey to happiness is easy."

In the carriage to the church, Mr Bennet told Elizabeth that the marriage settlement was very generous. "You shall be well cared for, my dear." His daughter could not look him in the eyes and stared out the carriage window. The journey was both too short and too long.

Elizabeth entered the church on her father's arm too humiliated and sad to raise her eyes to see her family and a few friends sitting in the front pews. Mr Bennet had to nudge his reluctant daughter to the altar where the waiting groom stared straight ahead. The parson, an amiable man with a bent towards jocularity, was unusually solemn and gave each in turn a look of concern. Mr Bennet nodded to him to continue so he did, saying, "Dearly beloved, we are gathered together here in the sight of God..."

The wedding ceremony was over quickly. Mr Darcy muttered his vows without ever so much as looking at Elizabeth, and Elizabeth felt tears sting her eyes while she said hers. The tears brought with them a faint twinge of guilt. How could she stand in the sight of God making promises that seemed impossible to keep?

When the ceremony was over and the registry had been signed, Mr Darcy took Elizabeth by the elbow and propelled her down the aisle. Outside the church, the few friends and family in attendance expressed their best wishes for Elizabeth's happiness while her new husband stood nearby and said nothing in response to their kind words. A few minutes later, the bride was seated in the waiting carriage. Mr Darcy did not afford his new wife the opportunity to properly farewell her family, and before she could understand what was happening, they were leaving Meryton.

Elizabeth was upset and frustrated at being rushed from the church and sitting opposite him in the carriage, asked angrily, "Mr Darcy, may I ask why I was not permitted time to say goodbye to all the wedding guests?"

"Since we are married, I would ask you to call me Fitzwilliam or Darcy when we are alone."

"And you may call me Elizabeth or Lizzy, and I would still like an answer."

Darcy, although affronted by her demand, did his best to keep a civil tone.

"Our journey to Pemberley is long, and we must keep

to our schedule if we are going to arrive in three days. It is time for the spring planting, and I must be there to assist my steward. I shall call you Lizzy when I know you better."

She does not know that my steward oversees the spring planting and that I was planning to stay with Bingley for a month. I could never have imagined that three weeks after stepping foot in Hertfordshire, I would be married to a local country girl.

"Pemberley is a working farm, and we and our tenants rely on a bountiful harvest in the fall. As to your friends, I had thought you would have spoken to them all before you left Longbourn this morning."

"No, I did not. I thought there would be ample opportunity to do so after the ceremony. My father told me about your reasons for not having a wedding breakfast, and I believe you were correct about having nothing to celebrate."

"Then I hope you will understand my desire not to be forced to stand outside the church and amiably accept the congratulations of your family and friends any longer than necessary."

Darcy could see the tears in his new wife's eyes but could scarcely credit them. *If there is anyone in this carriage who ought to weep, it is I. She should be celebrating her new position in society and everything that comes with it. I am married to someone far beneath me— someone who will never be acceptable to my relations or among the* ton. *My father taught me it was my duty to behave as a gentleman should. He said I must never disgrace the Darcy name or what it stands for. I am happy my parents are not alive to see how low I have fallen.*

The letter he had written to Georgiana telling her all about his wife had been full of feigned optimism and false hopes. How could he have told his sister he had no idea who his wife was and that he did not care? But Georgiana had long wished for a sister and her reply had been enthusiastic and dear.

'I am sure, Brother, that if you love her, then I shall love her dearly as well! I look forward to becoming true sisters of the heart as well as intimate friends.'

He grimaced. *I hope they become friends and I can spend as little time with this...this woman as possible.*

Across the carriage, Elizabeth had finally composed herself. She was staring out the window, evidently lost in thought, and Darcy took a moment to really look at her. He had initially dismissed any notion of beauty, but today he could see the appeal of her. She had lovely thick dark hair and eyes which shone with intelligence. Her figure was light and pleasing.

I must look for what is good in her, else I shall never survive this.

He took a breath and began to speak. "We are bound for Pemberley, my estate in Derbyshire. I will be busy with estate business, and you will learn how to be the mistress of a large manor house and estate. I expect you to visit our tenants and the vicar of Kympton and respond appropriately to the needs of the parishioners and cottagers."

Elizabeth nodded her acceptance to her new responsibilities.

"There is one more thing I need to clarify regarding the terms of our marriage," he added brusquely.

She looked startled. "What do you mean? My father told me you were very generous in the marriage settlements, for which I thank you."

"Not *that*." Darcy shook his head. "What I mean is that while we are travelling and stopping at inns along the road, we will sleep in separate rooms. When we arrive at Pemberley, I shall not expect you to come to me until you feel you are ready. I believe we should get to know each other better, but you should know that as my wife, you are responsible for producing my heir. For appearance's sake, you shall stay in the mistress's apartments, but the door between our rooms will be locked."

"I understand, and I thank you for your consideration," she said quietly.

"There is one more thing."

Looking at him as though expecting the worse, she replied, "What is it?"

"You must never wear one of those awful matron's caps. I find them very unattractive."

She nodded. "That is something upon which we agree."

After riding in silence for another half an hour, Elizabeth spoke. "You signed the church registry as

Fitzwilliam Darcy. I have never heard that Christian name."

"It was my mother's maiden name. She was born Lady Anne Fitzwilliam and I was her first and only son. It is a tradition in my family to name our sons thus." *And it is a tradition that will be broken with us because my son will never be called Bennet.*

"I see."

Darcy said nothing more. He retrieved a book from the leather valise in the carriage and used it to fix his attentions and avoid his wife. He had a feeling he would be doing the same very often in the future.

A few hours later, as they entered the carriage after a brief stop for a light repast, Darcy forced himself to make some attempt to get to know his wife better and asked her, "Do you like to read?"

"I do," she answered.

"Novels?" he asked with one brow raised.

"I have read quite a few of them, although I read poetry, the classics, and more serious works as well. I read anything, really."

This was a source of some relief to him. At least he could speak of books to her, although no doubt she would expect to make free use of the library at Pemberley. Was it his business to decide what she read? He decided on the spot that he did not care. If it kept her occupied and away from him, so be it.

"Can you play any instruments, draw, paint, speak other languages? When did your governess leave you?"

"We never had a governess."

"Never had a governess? With... How many sisters do you have?"

"My father has five daughters. Of us all, I was the one who most loved to learn."

"Are you saying your father superintended your education?" he asked incredulously.

"At times, yes, he did. He may not have had the means of a more affluent man, but he taught me all the things he would have taught his son, if in a somewhat haphazard way."

Darcy closed his eyes a moment, attempting to quell the dismay that rose within him. He had married a lady of no fortune, no breeding, and evidently no education either.

"Though my formal education may have been lacking, I do speak three languages, can read Latin, and have studied history, political science, geography, poetry, and philosophy. I have read all the authors my father deemed necessary to be considered well educated. I often acted as his clerk and took care of the estate records. I have settled disputes between our tenants and have tended to those in need in our parish. I play the pianoforte, though perhaps not as well as I could have if I had been more diligent in my practice, and I sing fairly well. I have no artistic talent whatsoever, I fear. Does that answer your questions?"

This reply mollified him a little. If she had truly applied herself to such an array of subjects, she should be able to hold her own against any seminary-educated female. At least she would not be accused of being a bluestocking! *She thinks herself well educated, but the truth of it will be revealed over time.*

"Yes. I thank you."

"And you?" she asked.

"Me?" He stared at her, seeking signs of intended impertinence. "You wish to know about my education?"

"You wished to hear about mine." She looked at him, seeming earnest, but he could scarcely credit that. "I wish to hear of yours as well."

"I had a gentleman's education," he replied stiffly. "I had an excellent governess in my earliest years, then came to London with my father to be instructed by a gentleman there until I was thirteen or so, when I went to Eton, then Cambridge for university."

"And what did you—"

He interrupted her. "Do you ride? I have a fine stable full of horses."

She paused a moment, then said, "As you so clearly witnessed, I prefer long walks." With a slight smile, she added, "I have never been much of a horsewoman."

"By the by, I have given this a great deal of thought, and I think it best we do not tell anyone of the circumstances of our marriage. The fewer people who know the truth, the better."

Just then, the carriage was jostled. Hot pain tore through Darcy, and he grabbed his side, grimacing. When he saw Elizabeth's genuine look of concern, he explained, "I have some pain from the injury I suffered when we were thrown from my horse. It seems I broke several ribs, and my physician in London wrapped my midsection to minimise my movements. He said it could be many weeks before I am without discomfort."

Sincerity shone from her eyes, and she leant forward saying, "I am sorry you were injured trying to help me."

Her tenderness could only soften him, and he nearly smiled as he said, "I am sorry my actions resulted in us being forced to wed, but I was only doing what I thought best at the time. I have ridden Apollo for years, through all kinds of weather, and he has never before reacted to lightning that way."

"There is no reason to apologise. You are suffering from our accident as much as I," replied Elizabeth. "I could have insisted more fervently that we not ride together, but as unhappy as I was with the idea of sitting atop your horse with you, I realised, finally, that it was best to get out of the storm and cooperate with your scheme."

"And I daresay I ought to have listened to you and allowed you to go on your way. It certainly would have been to the benefit of both of us." He sighed deeply.

"I only wanted to return home as quickly as possible." She shrugged. "But these reflections do us no good. It is done, and perhaps the best thing for us to do is to put in the past the events that brought us to this situation."

He nodded. "That is good advice. We are married

now, and there is no sense chafing over what could have been done or what might have been done."

They had ridden in silence for thirty minutes or more when Elizabeth spoke. "I was surprised when Taylor arrived with my new clothes."

During the brief days of their acquaintance, Darcy had observed the inferior quality of his wife's wardrobe and had written to his aunt, Lady Matlock, in London and asked that, in addition to the small travelling wardrobe, she would order day dresses and dinner gowns for the same young woman. Before leaving town for his wedding, he asked his aunt to order more dresses and gowns and to have Georgiana bring them with her when she travelled north to Pemberley. At the same time, he had sent Fitzwilliam a letter with the news of his marriage since his cousin would meet Elizabeth when he arrived with Georgiana. He asked Fitzwilliam to keep the news to himself, as Darcy was not yet prepared for anyone in town to learn of his sham marriage.

"Surely you must have expected that Mrs Darcy would have her own lady's maid?"

"I had not given it much thought, in truth. The new clothes, however, I could not have anticipated."

He repeated the prevarication that he had made with his instructions to the maid. "My sister, Georgiana, wanted you to have some new things since there was no time for you to purchase your trousseau."

"It is very good of her to think of me. As you know, everything has happened so quickly." After a short pause, she added, "In truth, I did only a little shopping in Meryton with my mother and my sister Jane. I have never been one to enjoy the shops."

"Then you will be glad to hear I have enlisted the help of my aunt, Lady Matlock, in selecting more new gowns for you. My sister will bring them with her to Pemberley."

"Oh! There is no need for anyone else to go to any trouble on my behalf. I do not care—"

"Care or care not, it is important that you look as Mrs Darcy should," he warned.

The flash of anger in her expression made clear to Darcy that she did not like his interruption, but it did not signify. She had to learn that her country-town indifference to things carried no weight with him or anyone else of his circle. "London is quite different from Meryton, and the *ton* can be merciless in their judgments of those from the outside," he said firmly.

"How unfortunate," she replied in a cool voice. "I vastly prefer to judge people on their character rather than on the gown they are wearing."

Darcy did not know how to respond to her comment. Surely, she must understand that her new place in society, indeed her entire life, would be different from what she had known in her girlhood? He prayed she understood, for if she did not... He shuddered to imagine it. She could not allow her country ways to precede her.

"Your role as Mrs Darcy will become clearer to you after we arrive in Derbyshire. Our housekeeper, Mrs

Reynolds, has served my family for many years and can help teach you what you will need to know to be a proper mistress of Pemberley. Your maid will help you learn how you should look and how to conduct yourself in town."

To this, she made no reply.

When the sun began to set, they stopped at a lovely inn. They ate dinner in silence within a private parlour and climbed the stairs to their chambers at different times. When her maid was helping her mistress prepare for bed, she asked, "Pardon me, madam, but will Mr Darcy be joining you tonight?"

Fearing that Taylor had heard some of the vile rumours circulating in Meryton, Elizabeth snapped at her maid, "Why are you asking me that?"

"I thought you might like to wear one of your new nightgowns."

"No, that will not be necessary." She paused to calm herself and considered her next words carefully. "In fact, pray do not ask me that question again until I tell you otherwise."

"Yes, Mrs Darcy. I understand. Goodnight."

Though neither knew it of the other, Darcy and Elizabeth equally dreaded the long hours of silence in the carriage and had thus brought several books to read. Although no words were exchanged, Darcy soon realised that their taste in reading material was quite similar. He found himself pleased by what she was reading and found himself hoping that it might be something shared between them. *My wife might not be the ignorant country girl I initially feared I had married.*

As she appeared to be quite absorbed in what she read, Darcy allowed himself to study her. *She does have lovely expressive eyes and is rather pretty in an unconventional way. Her shapely figure is evidently due to her love of walking. Her scent...I believe it is jasmine. Or at least hints of it.*

The subject of the book she was reading—botany and agriculture in the northern counties—was not one generally enjoyed by ladies. Was she trying to learn about Derbyshire? The thought was undeniably flattering.

She may be as well read as she claimed. I am confident she could discuss a wide variety of works, both novels and historical books, if I had the desire.

"You will enjoy the library at Pemberley," he said abruptly. "It is the work of many generations, and the collection is quite large. You may feel free to take any volume you would like to read."

Elizabeth looked at him with a half-smile on her face and nodded her thanks, then returned to her reading.

Darcy raised his own book, feigning reading but in truth continuing to watch Elizabeth read, a contrariety of feelings stirring within him. He had begun in impassioned dislike. He was undeniably bitter that she was now his wife, that a few minutes in a field had led to the exact circumstance he had always striven to avoid. *There was no one I have ever wished to marry, but I was biding my time until I met an appropriate young woman with whom I had something in common—someone from my social circle, someone with connexions, and someone with a dowry!*

He had softened a little the day prior, recognising the good in her, but as he had lain awake in the hard bed at the inn, all his fears and concerns had come rushing back to him. While he might have found some small things to like about her, he surely did not love her, nor could he imagine he ever would. She was wholly unsuitable, and he would never forget what had come about to force him into this situation. That resentment would not be forgotten.

She noticed him looking at her. "You have met, albeit briefly, my family. Will you tell me about yours? I have heard you have a sister, and your parents are gone. Is your remaining family circle large?"

Darcy quelled the urge to tell her that if she had not

married him, she should never have known such exalted people as his relations and instead said, "You shall meet Georgiana next week. She is being escorted to Pemberley by my cousin, Colonel Richard Fitzwilliam. He shares guardianship of her with me."

"I shall look forward to meeting them both. Do you have many other cousins? What about your aunts and uncles?"

"You need not concern yourself with the rest of my family. There are currently no plans for you to meet them."

His words were too harsh. Darcy saw the hurt look on his wife's face, but he could not console her. He could not deny the truth, that until he knew she could become a proper wife for him, he was not willing to let his relations know what a mistake their marriage was.

Their days on the road passed slowly. They rarely spoke and then only when necessary to discuss the plans for stopping. Their trip had been unaffected by weather; the roads were dry, and Elizabeth hoped their silent journey would soon be over. There had been some all-too-brief moments of warmth between them, times that hinted at an accord, but after each of these, her husband grew more resentful and snappish, then retreated even further into his silence. It was plain to Elizabeth that not only did he dislike her, but he also seemed to want to nurture his discontent.

It was not her way. She had never been formed for ill humour, and she did not intend to begin now. She would make the best of this, no matter what, and could only hope he would eventually come around. *I pray there is someone I can talk to at Pemberley! After the happy, continuous chatter of Longbourn, it is quite difficult to bear these heavy silences.*

Late on the afternoon of the third day of travel, they entered a thick wood, and when the trees thinned, she saw an enormous stone house fronted by a stream feeding into a lake which reflected the manor house in the afternoon sun. Elizabeth was amazed by the beauty of it and—if she was honest—more than a little awed to imagine herself mistress of such a place.

So, this is Pemberley. I never imagined Mr Darcy was so wealthy as this.

Some minutes later, the carriage stopped in front of the manor house and a footman helped Elizabeth descend. She was warmly greeted by an older woman whom Darcy introduced as Mrs Reynolds, the house-keeper of long tenure. She greeted Elizabeth with thinly disguised curiosity as well as a little surprise. Elizabeth did not doubt that she was not what the lady might have expected of a new mistress.

As they entered the house, some of the servants were lined up to welcome her, and she tried to be as sincere as possible while Mrs Reynolds made the introductions to them. Darcy stood to the side and waited for the process to end. When the servants were dismissed, he said, "Mrs Reynolds, kindly show Mrs Darcy to her chambers. I must attend to a few matters in my study." He looked at Elizabeth and added, "I will join you later for dinner."

If Mrs Reynolds was surprised by his brusque manner towards his new bride, she gave no indication of it. "This way, madam."

After climbing the grand staircase, they began to walk down a long corridor, their footsteps making no sound on the plush carpet. "I made a few changes to your rooms, only to freshen them up, you see. It has been some time since a lady was in residence in those apartments, so we did what we could to bring a breath of air into them, but there was such a short time to prepare, we could only do so much. Of course, you must make any changes you wish."

"Thank you, ma'am. I am sure they are lovely," Elizabeth replied.

The walk to reach her rooms was not inconsiderable but Elizabeth found herself alternately pleased and dismayed by all she saw—pleased because it was a beautiful house with none of the gaudiness or useless finery of many great houses; dismayed because with every step she recognised she found herself in a different world, a place she did not belong. *And I suspect my husband will not allow me to forget that.*

After her tour of her chambers, Elizabeth found herself alone as Taylor unpacked her things in her dressing room, and it was then that the distress of her situation hit her in full. She inspected the fine furniture, fabrics, and art which adorned the walls of her bed chamber. Her suite of rooms was what young women dream about their entire lives, but nothing she saw could take away the anxiety she felt so acutely. There was a lovely sitting room adjoining her and her husband's chambers, but she did not anticipate they would be spending any time there together.

I have never been mercenary. These fine furnishings and elegant gowns will never be an adequate substitute for friendship, respect, and love.

Taylor helped her dress for dinner and took special care styling her hair. "You look lovely, Mrs Darcy. Is there anything else I can do for you?"

"I believe that is all for now save for one thing. Can you tell me where I am going?"

"Indeed, the Darcys meet in the drawing room before dining." The maid gave her excellent directions and, with the exception of one wrong turn, the new Mrs Darcy soon found herself standing in the doorway of the drawing room. She found her husband pacing between the high windows on either side of the fireplace.

He spotted her as she walked into the room and ceased his restive steps. "Good evening. Would you like some wine?"

"No, thank you," Elizabeth replied with a smile. She hoped, rather than believed, that if things began pleasantly, they would continue thus.

"We should go into dinner now."

Darcy offered his arm and led her into a small dining room but left a footman to help seat her as he took his place on the other side of the large table. *Clearly, he does not intend to speak much to me, unless we are to shout to one another.*

The soup course was on the table immediately, hot and savoury, and Elizabeth sipped at it in silence. It was followed by the meat course, which the butler brought and served to her. Although Mrs Bennet had always set a fine table at Longbourn, the food was richer than Elizabeth was accustomed to for a family dinner.

She wished she could more fully enjoy the delicious food, but her stomach was in knots. Each successive mouthful seemed to bring with it a new worry. *What shall I do here at Pemberley? How will I pass my days?* She wished to be an active and useful mistress, but she suspected Darcy would rather she remained hidden away.

Will he come to my room tonight? He said he would wait until we know each other better. He cannot mean that the few words we exchanged in the carriage would qualify.

At length, careful to keep her tone light, she

proposed, "After dinner, do you think I could have a brief tour of the house? I had to ask my maid how to find you this evening."

Darcy did not raise his eyes from his plate. "Mrs Reynolds will be happy to show you around tomorrow. Just ask her to limit the number of rooms she shows you each day. It can be quite overwhelming until you get accustomed to the house."

That attempt at conversation failed, and Elizabeth returned to her plate, although she found the food was now quite tasteless to her.

Alone in bed that night, Elizabeth stared at the floral canopy above her and thought about everything that had happened in the past three weeks. *I was an innocent young woman going out for a walk, and here I am, still innocent, but a married woman who lives in the largest, most beautiful house I could ever imagine. I have only seen three of the downstairs rooms, and there is so much more to discover. I will have to draw myself a map, so I do not embarrass myself by getting lost. I would not want to give Mr Darcy another reason to disdain his wife.*

Elizabeth did her best to situate herself in her new home. She learnt to navigate the many halls and staircases of the manor house and began meeting with Mrs

Reynolds every day to find ways to fill her hours productively. Elizabeth learnt more about the estate, their tenants, the crops that were grown on their properties, their orchards, and their livestock. She was shown the estate's ledgers which related to the running of the house, the ordering of supplies for the kitchen, and the planning of the dinner menus.

"You are a very quick learner, Mrs Darcy," Mrs Reynolds said approvingly. "In a few weeks, you will be able to take charge of the meal planning, and I will be happy for you to assume that responsibility."

"Thank you, ma'am. I confess, Pemberley is a much larger and more complex estate than the one I was raised at. I used to help my father with our estate books, but Longbourn is so much smaller that I feel I am acquiring many new skills. My mother did most of the menu planning, so I am learning some things for the first time."

"Your mother and father seem to have prepared you well. Most of it just comes with time," Mrs Reynolds said warmly. "I am so delighted Mr Darcy married you. You bring so much happiness to the house, and I daresay you are just what we need here."

Ignoring her last comment, Elizabeth said, "Thank you, Mrs Reynolds. Your help has been invaluable to me."

"We are all very happy to have you here, Mrs Darcy. The master and Miss Georgiana have been very lonely since their parents left us. It is good to have some felicity restored to the house."

"Pemberley is simply beautiful. Who would not be

happy here?" Elizabeth replied, knowing her words were nothing more than artful disguise.

Who would not be happy here? Me! I am exceedingly lonely and unhappy! Over the course of a day, my husband barely says two words to me, and that is only when someone else is in the room. I keep hoping I will wake up from this horrible dream and find myself back in my bed at Longbourn with Jane snoring beside me!

Four

Every morning since arriving at Pemberley, Elizabeth entered an empty breakfast room and ate her meal in silence. Her husband often left his newspapers on the table, and she used this time to catch up on the news from London. After the first few days, a footman left the discarded periodicals next to her plate. She did not see Darcy until she met him in the drawing room in the evening and he escorted her to another dinner eaten in near silence.

At least my husband was right about his library. It is beyond anything I could imagine, and I have already picked out several books I have wished to read. When I was at Longbourn, how I prayed for some quiet. Now I almost feel like screaming simply to hear my own voice.

My time with Mrs Reynolds has been very beneficial. I can now navigate most of the house without getting lost. We have inspected all the guest rooms for any changes that they may need. There are so many things I would like to discuss with Darcy, but he has made it clear to me that he is not interested in anything I have to say.

Darcy woke early every morning and, after a quick breakfast, rode out with his steward. They inspected the fields and made note of areas that needed more water or better drainage. Each time they encountered one of the tenants in the field, the tenant congratulated him on his marriage and expressed best wishes to him and the new Mrs Darcy, which he attempted to accept with equanimity. When he was at home, he kept himself busy working on estate business and letters to his family. He tried not to let thoughts of his new wife interrupt his responsibilities to Pemberley.

While he was out riding, however, Darcy had too much time to think about the woman now living in his home and the radical changes she brought to his life. *My wife is a very curious person, always asking questions which I have no desire to answer. I fear if I talk to her too much, she will get the wrong idea and think I want to spend time with her and share my thoughts with her. I imagine that is what most married people do, but the circumstances which led to our marriage were so unexpected, I cannot yet think of her as a partner, someone I wish to be a part of my life. I can only pray that someday I will feel differently about her.*

When Elizabeth had been living in Derbyshire for little more than a fortnight, she was summoned to join Darcy outside on the front steps. She stood silently near her husband while a gentleman in regimentals bearing the marks of a colonel exited a carriage. He then turned to help an elegant young woman step down. Following her came a middle-aged woman, dressed simply but neatly, who thanked the colonel for his assistance.

Darcy walked quickly towards them, lovingly embraced the young lady, and shook hands with the colonel. The man in uniform stepped towards Elizabeth and bowed, looking at Darcy expectantly when he rose.

In a voice devoid of nearly all feeling, Darcy said, "Mrs Darcy, may I present to you my cousin, Colonel Richard Fitzwilliam, and my sister, Miss Georgiana Darcy."

The colonel was not a handsome man, but he was made handsomer by his mode of address, which was gentlemanly and kind. "It is very good to meet you, Mrs Darcy," he said warmly. "It is about time my cousin finally settled down, though being younger than I am, he might accuse me of the same!"

Elizabeth laughed politely then turned to her new sister, shocked when the younger girl embraced her with enthusiasm. "I am so happy to meet you, Mrs Darcy. I have waited so long to have a sister of my own, and now I do!"

Elizabeth recovered from her surprise in time to return the girl's hug. In truth, the warmth of it, after so many weeks of cold hauteur, was balm to her wounded spirits, and the relief nearly made her lose her composure. "I am delighted to meet you as well," she managed to say. "But pray call me Elizabeth or Lizzy as my other sisters do."

"Then you must call me Georgiana, as well," the girl said with a beaming smile and another tight embrace. "May I introduce you to my companion, Mrs Annesley."

Mrs Annesley curtseyed. "I am delighted to make your acquaintance, Mrs Darcy."

"And I yours. Let us all go into the drawing room for some refreshments." Elizabeth led the group into the house, presuming that her husband would follow.

After sharing tea, the men withdrew to Darcy's study and Mrs Annesley went to her chambers to rest. Georgiana and Elizabeth remained together speaking of inconsequential things for several minutes. Elizabeth was hungry for this sort of talk, the easy camaraderie between young ladies, but she soon recognised that Georgiana might also need to rest. "You must be tired from your journey, Georgiana. Would you like to retire to your rooms before dinner?"

"Yes, I am a bit fatigued. You are so kind to think of my comfort. I shall see you at dinner." Georgiana rose and then bent, giving Elizabeth a swift kiss on the cheek before she left.

Heartened by the kindness of her new relations, Elizabeth decided that before she returned to her chambers, she would ask the colonel if he had any special requests for dinner while he was with them. As she rose, she realised her face felt odd. Evidently, she had grown so out of the practise of smiling that her cheeks now ached from having smiled so much in an hour's time.

Putting aside that gloomy thought, Elizabeth went down the hall to where the men sat. The door was ajar as she approached Darcy's study, and she stopped walking as she overheard the men discussing her.

"Your wife is lovely, but I do not believe I ever heard you mention her name before. Were you keeping your courtship a secret?"

For a moment, her husband did not reply, finally saying, "There was no courtship. We had an accident and afterwards were found together by her father and some neighbours."

Darcy then told his cousin the truth about it all, holding nothing back regarding his feelings for the matter. Elizabeth felt her face go aflame listening to his spite pouring forth. It was nothing she had not known or suspected, of course, but to hear it stated so baldly was still distressing.

The colonel offered the appropriate consolations to his cousin. "You will have to make of it what you can. It is done—you married her. Georgiana told me she is a gentleman's daughter, at least. That is a comfort."

"A small comfort. Her father has a small estate; however, from what little I saw of him, he is too indolent to make any effort to make more than the most minimal profit from his holdings. From what I hear, they over-spend their income at every turn."

The colonel chuckled. "You do not find much to admire in your new relations."

"My wife has relatives in trade. She came with no fortune of her own, and, needless to say, she has no connexion to anyone of consequence. Her entire family's behaviour is unsuitable. Mrs Darcy's mother does nothing to restrain the inappropriate behaviour of her youngest daughters. They chase after anyone who will flirt with them—the youngest is already out in society, and she is but fifteen! Her mother speaks of nothing but pushing her daughters towards any eligible man who looks their way. If I did not know better, I would accuse Mrs Bennet of causing the bolt of lightning that caused my horse to rear."

Elizabeth's hand rose to her mouth, silencing her gasp. She could not believe what she was hearing: her husband divulging the details of their betrothal after they had mutually agreed to tell no one and then further speaking of her family in such disparaging terms.

It was a severe blow, particularly coming so hard on the heels of her nascent good feelings engendered from meeting the colonel and Georgiana. She wanted to run but paused a moment, hearing the colonel respond.

"You have been the object of many an avaricious matchmaking mama—some with much more at stake than the daughter of a modest country gentlemen. Family and situation aside, I think you must own that she did not intend to entrap you, Darcy. You can hardly blame your wife for the unexpected accident that led to all of this."

"Nevertheless, one cannot deny that in marrying her, I have lost as much as she has gained."

"She probably had no idea of your wealth until she arrived here. By the by, my mother told me to bring the gowns you requested she purchase on your behalf." The colonel's voice took on a teasing tone, "As she has no idea that you are married, I daresay she thinks they are for your mistress!"

Her husband did not betray any amusement at that thought. "The gowns I saw her wearing before our wedding did not befit my wife, and at the time, I told her that the clothes were a gift from Georgiana since Elizabeth had no time to acquire her trousseau."

"I mentioned that to Georgiana and although she did not understand why, she agreed to go along with your scheme. Darcy, I can see how unhappy you are, and I am in no position to give advice."

"But you shall anyway."

"True. But from what I have observed in my travels, felicity in marriage is a matter of chance. Contentment, however, is a matter of choice. Something to admire can be found in most people, and if you treat someone kindly, that kindness will be returned. You do not need great passion to have a good life. Have you ever felt passion for any of the ladies you danced with at Almack's with all their fortunes and connexions?"

"You know the answer to that question."

"Then I suggest you think about what you want and do not fret for what you think you might have lost."

There was a pause until finally Darcy said, "When I am ready to follow your advice, what do I do if she rebuffs my attempts to be kind?"

"You must keep trying. The woman is your wife."

"I shall think about what you have said. No matter how I feel, nothing will change the fact that we are married." Darcy expelled a great sigh. "Thank you, Cousin. Perhaps you are becoming wiser in your old age."

They both laughed.

Having heard much more than she ought, Elizabeth turned slowly, careful to be silent, and then raced up the stairs with hot tears running down her face. *He has betrayed my trust. We agreed not to tell anyone the circumstances leading to our marriage! I hate him for his arrogance and pride. I hate him for thinking he may treat me as he likes until he is 'ready to be kind'.*

Elizabeth was still crying when she entered her room and saw all the boxes and packages piled on her loveseat. "More clothes from Miss Darcy, ma'am. Shall I unpack them?"

Elizabeth nodded her head and Taylor, no doubt realising her mistress was quite upset, added, "You can try them on tomorrow, and I can make any alterations they may need."

Elizabeth could not stop crying and asked her maid to thank Georgiana for the clothes and tell her that she had a terrible headache and would not be joining them for dinner.

"Where were you this morning, Elizabeth?" Darcy asked his wife sternly the following day.

"I beg your pardon. What do you mean?"

"Taylor said you were not in your chambers this morning, and no one knew where you were."

"I left the house early to go for a walk."

"Madam, you are the mistress of Pemberley. You are not to be so careless as to walk unescorted, especially when it is barely daylight. You are never to walk alone again. You are to have a footman with you no matter the hour. Do you understand?"

Darcy's clenched fists on the table could clearly be seen by his cousin and Georgiana; they looked at their plates as Darcy chastised his wife. When he finished speaking, Elizabeth rose, curtseyed deeply to her husband, and left the room.

"Brother, how could you speak so harshly to Lizzy?"

"Harshly? Were you not as worried about her whereabouts as everyone else in the house?"

"Yes, but don't you think your concern could have been expressed to her in a more private setting?"

"Perhaps, but I will not risk her being injured or abducted while she is away from the house."

"Brother, I never thought you could be so cruel—and to your own wife!" Georgiana rose and left the table.

Darcy looked at Richard, who returned his glance with one of disapproval as he shook his head. "You know, Darcy, you could learn a lot from your sister. From now on, tell her what you are planning to say to Mrs Darcy, and she can keep you from further insulting your wife. I want nothing more for you than to find happiness and contentment in your life. Mrs Darcy is an attractive, spirited young woman and I wish you would listen to my advice: be kinder to your wife. Pray try it before I return to London."

Elizabeth spent the remainder of the day in her chambers, sending Georgiana a note telling her that her headache had returned but she planned to join everyone for dinner. That evening, Elizabeth, adorned in one of her new gowns with her hair fashioned in the latest style, stared at her reflection in the mirror. She could not deny that her appearance was fashionable and beautiful, or that it was far superior to any other gown she had ever owned. Nevertheless, she hated what it represented—

hated that it had come about because of her husband's disgust of who she was.

She gathered her courage as she descended the stairs and hoped she appeared almost cheerful as she joined the rest of their party in the drawing room before dinner.

Georgiana was seated in a chair near to the door and smiled happily at her. "Brother, just look at Lizzy! Do you not think she looks uncommonly beautiful tonight?"

Darcy walked towards her and offered a brief bow and a smile. To his sister he said, "Yes, Georgiana, Mrs Darcy looks quite lovely, indeed."

"Your aunt has excellent taste," Elizabeth replied. "Perhaps I may meet her someday to compliment her on it and thank her for her help."

That idea made Darcy's smile slip a bit, but Elizabeth knew not if either Georgiana or the colonel noticed. Her husband was studying her in a way she found disconcerting. Accustomed as she was to his scorn, approbation— or what she believed might be approbation—could only unsettle her.

As they were walking to the dining room, Elizabeth saw her husband wince, and his hand rose to touch his side. "I fear your ribs continue to plague you."

Immediately realising her error in referring to the accident which precipitated their marriage, Elizabeth covered her mistake by turning to Georgiana, who was walking behind them on the colonel's arm. "Your brother had an unfortunate fall when he tried to impress me with his ability to jump over one of the stone walls surrounding Longbourn."

"I am much better, but I need to continue to wrap my ribs for another few weeks. Thank you for asking."

"Brother!" Georgiana exclaimed. "You are usually very good at jumping."

"This was a particularly high wall," Darcy replied shortly.

From there, dinner was pleasant. Elizabeth had taken advantage of having two additional persons at the table to bring them closer together, and conversation flowed apace. Her new sister was shy but would come out of her shell with just a little prompting, and the colonel was affable enough to make even his dour cousin smile and laugh. It was a pity his visit would be of short duration, but Georgiana's permanent company was welcome indeed.

After breakfast the next morning, Georgiana asked Elizabeth to take a walk outside. Elizabeth happily agreed, and the two ladies set off on a tour of the grounds closest to the house. Elizabeth marvelled at the number of scenic walking paths and the contrast between the beautiful formal gardens and the untamed natural vege-tation that grew around the manor. "It is so beautiful, and soon everything will be in bloom. I can only imagine the colours! The roses will be magnificent in another month."

"Roses were my mother's favourite flower, and she designed this rose garden herself," Georgiana explained. "Every mistress of the house has planted some sort of garden or area to reflect her personal preferences. I expect you will do the same?"

"Oh! Well, I had not known of that custom." Elizabeth smiled at her sister, thinking of how little Darcy would want her making alterations to his home.

"What is your favourite flower? I confess I am quite partial to gardenias, but that is hardly unique."

Elizabeth laughed. "I suppose I would say I enjoy roses too. I have always thought there was some metaphor for life in them. They are beautiful and fragrant, but the possibility for pain lies very close."

Georgiana seemed not to know what to say to this disclosure. Smiling, she said, "I am so happy you are here. You will love living at Pemberley."

"I cannot imagine a more beautiful home."

At least that is the truth, if only there was happiness within it for me!

Five

June 1812

The chill of spring lingered longer in Derbyshire than it customarily did in Hertfordshire but nevertheless, the days grew longer, sunshine was more frequent, and the air grew redolent with the earthy scent of renewed life in the fields and gardens.

Elizabeth kept herself busy, knowing that if she had too much idle time, she would only wallow in her unhappiness. And she was, indeed, unhappy. Her husband did not want her and, in fact, disdained her. She saw it in his every look, word, and deed.

Nevertheless, she would find contentment such as she could and, to that end, resolved to make herself useful in her new home. She began a routine whereby she walked early every morning, and after breakfast she met with Mrs Reynolds to discuss the dinner menus and learn more about the running of Pemberley. One day, the housekeeper suggested Mrs Darcy introduce herself to some of their tenants and get to know them—an idea Elizabeth readily agreed to. As she was departing, Darcy was leaving his study and asked where she was going.

"I am going to introduce myself to some of the tenants."

"May I join you?"

Surprised by his question, she tried to sound calm as she replied, "Of course. The carriage is waiting outside."

After a short journey during which they did not speak, Elizabeth entered the Webber home with Darcy behind her. A moment later, a small girl ran towards her, and instinctively, Elizabeth scooped her up in her arms. "What is your name, pretty miss?"

Elizabeth felt some immediate relief to her low spirits to be among the children of the tenants. They seemed to warm to her naturally, and she was as comfortable among them as she was with the tenants of Longbourn. Several times, she found Darcy's critical eye upon her, and he stared at her nearly the whole way back to Pemberley. She did her best to ignore his notice, imagining she had likely displeased him in some way but unsure how.

Darcy could not deny that the ease and friendliness with which Elizabeth had gone about the estate had warmed him. A small piece of the stone that encased his heart had fallen away. Part of him wished to resist it, but he realised that to do so was foolish. Her caring instincts were clearly demonstrated while visiting the tenants, and her intelligent responses to their questions forced him to admire his wife in a way he had previously thought impossible.

The following morning, Darcy was outside his study door when he saw his wife descend the stairs and smile at Mrs Reynolds. "Good morning. I was hoping you might find some time for me today to review more of the household records."

"Of course, madam. Would ten o'clock suit?"

"Yes, I will meet you here at ten."

As he watched his wife walk towards the breakfast room, he thought, *At least she is trying to do her job as mistress of the house. How well she succeeds remains to be seen. She greeted the housekeeper warmly, and their relationship is critical to the success of Pemberley running well.*

As the season shifted to summer, Elizabeth continued to exchange only a few words a day with her husband and spend most of her time with Georgiana and Mrs Annesley. She sat in company with them in the music room or sat alone in her sitting room, reading or sewing. *My life could be worse, I suppose. I have many tasks as mistress, and helping the tenants and parishioners is very worthwhile. I enjoy my time with Georgiana, but surely, she*

must realise that all is not right between her brother and I.

At the dinner table, Georgiana and Elizabeth kept up a steady conversation while Darcy sat in his chair eating and listening. Many evenings, Elizabeth would turn to her husband and ask questions about something she had seen or heard about the estate. "Did the Webbers have their roof repaired?"

"I believe it has been taken care of."

"And the broken windows at the Mortons'?"

"They have been repaired."

My husband has no interest in talking to me. How many times must I make the first attempt to begin a conversation? Georgiana does not appear to realise her brother's abruptness with me or is too involved with her dinner to notice. I will keep trying but everyone has their limits.

The three ladies were gathered in the drawing room enjoying some tea and discussing the interpretation of Georgiana's recent English literature lessons. Elizabeth remarked, "If we always agreed with everyone else's thoughts about fiction or politics or anything else, what a dull world it would be."

Darcy stood in the doorway as Georgiana looked at Mrs Annesley and replied, "One of the things I most admire about Lizzy is that she has her own way of analysing things and always speaks her mind."

He entered the room at that moment, and Elizabeth rose to prepare tea for him. "I believe this is how you like it," she said as she handed him the cup.

Their hands touched briefly, and he watched her face as he took the tea-cup from her. "Yes, I thank you." He had observed her pour his cup and noted the care she took in preparing it precisely as he enjoyed it. He realised how hard she was trying to be a good wife, and his heart stirred a bit at the thought.

"Fitzwilliam," said Georgiana, "Mrs Annesley and I were discussing poetry today, and she showed me a poem that begins, 'God moves in a mysterious way'. Oh dear, now I am trying to remember who wrote it."

At the same time as his wife, Darcy replied, "William Cowper." Elizabeth gave him a mirthful glance which he returned with a small smile while the other two ladies laughed at the unison of their responses.

When Darcy returned to his study, he thought back on his interaction with his wife. *She is a kind, intelligent person who has helped my sister a great deal. We had an amicable exchange in the drawing room, and she was quick to respond to my sister's question. Perhaps poetry is something we have in common. It is up to me, I suppose, to find other similar interests we share.*

Before dressing for dinner that evening, Elizabeth sat at the escritoire in her chambers and thought about what had transpired in the drawing room with her husband and the moment of levity as they both answered Georgiana's query. She had been happily surprised by her husband's smile at her response. *He is very handsome when he is not scowling.*

Was she starting to see him in a different, more favourable light? Darcy was an educated, intelligent man, but he had yet to share more than a few words with her. She did not know much more now about the kind of person he was than she did on their wedding day. She hoped to have an intelligent, meaningful discussion with him one day. Elizabeth decided to write to her aunt, someone on whom she could depend to give her the best advice. She did not wish to worry her relations with the truth of how sad she was but wanted to inform them about her life in Derbyshire.

June 1812
    Pemberley, Derbyshire

Dear Aunt Gardiner,

I pray you will forgive me for not writing to you sooner. As you have undoubtedly learnt from my mother, I am lately married to Mr Fitzwilliam Darcy of Pemberley in Derbyshire. I am enjoying my life here, and I can well understand your love of this county. Every day I am learning more and more from the housekeeper about the running of this beautiful estate. My new sister, Georgiana, is a delightful young woman, and we already think of each other as sisters. She plays the pianoforte so much better than anyone I have ever heard before. We spend a great deal of time together along with Georgiana's companion, a lovely woman named Mrs Annesley. We often walk through the extensive gardens and along the scenic paths, and as the weather continues to get warmer, I have enjoyed more and more of my time out of doors.

Mr Darcy is always occupied. He often leaves the house before breakfast and does not return until dinner time. The estate is so vast, and he has many responsibilities. We are getting to know each other better every day, and I believe that our marriage can be a happy one. Indeed, I am determined to make it so. Just today we had a very pleasant afternoon sharing tea and discussing poetry. I have visited many of the tenants and the local vicar to see what must be done to meet their needs, and I will do whatever else is expected of me as the mistress of this estate.

Please send my love to your dear family,
    Elizabeth Darcy

July 1812
    Cheapside, London

Dearest Lizzy,

Congratulations on your marriage. Your father wrote to your uncle regarding the circumstances of your wedding and, while regrettable, it is surely done. You are far away from all that now, and it is up to you to adjust to the fact that you are now a married woman. Your common sense and good nature will ensure you find happiness and love as Mrs Darcy.

Your husband is a wonderful man, and I do not speak only of his position and means. If he is anything like his father, which my friends in Lambton tell me is the case, your Mr Darcy is a man of superior understanding and genuine charity to those less fortunate than himself. Try to break the ice between you and enjoy yourself. We all know how dearly you love to laugh. Your uncle and I will do anything we can to help you with your new duties, but the responsibility of getting to know your husband and make yours a marriage of affection, if not love, lies with you.

Jane wrote and told me that Mr Bingley has been a frequent caller at Longbourn. Am I wrong in suspecting that she has developed strong feelings for the man? I hope he will propose soon. I would be delighted to have my two favourite nieces so happily situated.

Your aunt,
  Madeline Gardiner

Elizabeth set down the letter, feeling heartened by what she had read.

How I wish you were here to talk to, my dear aunt. I will try to see things from your point of view, and I do hope to be happy in my marriage. But love? I doubt it. Elizabeth knew she had a naturally affectionate heart, but in the absence of any warmth whatsoever from Darcy, she thought even she was unequal to romance.

Six

Darcy slowly began to see his wife in a new light. He recognised her genuine care for his sister, which meant a great deal to him. Furthermore, he enjoyed her playful nature when he surreptitiously observed the two ladies practising duets together and admired her ability to discuss his sister's lessons intelligently. He could not deny she looked lovely when she came to dinner or that he had begun to think of her in ways that a man who was a husband in name only ought not. *I cannot allow myself to act on my attraction to her until I know how she feels about me.*

It was odd to consider her feelings in this. It made him aware of how little he had considered them in the past. He had initially expected her to be exulting, in the manner of her mother, over entrapping him, but she certainly did not seem to be. His wealth seemed to matter rather little, and while she often seemed complacent and cheerful, his understanding of her wit began to make him think her high spirits were no more than a façade. While they sat at the dinner table, he admired how pretty she was and how the candlelight enhanced the gold and red highlights in her chestnut hair and made her eyes sparkle with life.

At breakfast the following morning, Darcy asked his sister what she had scheduled for the day. "Lizzy and I are planning to go to Lambton to do some shopping. As mistress of Pemberley, it is time she was introduced to the local shops and merchants to whom we give our custom."

"That is a very good idea. Would you ladies mind if I joined you? I need to pick up a few things from town."

"Of course you may come with us." Georgiana asked teasingly, "Lizzy, do you mind if your husband joins us?"

"Not at all. He is a most welcome addition to our shopping party."

A few hours later, after they had arrived back at Pemberley from shopping, Darcy sat in his study thinking about their trip to Lambton. Elizabeth had been very kind to all the merchants and accepted congratulations on their marriage with a genuine smile. She carefully inspected everything she purchased but had made an effort to buy something in every shop they visited— even if it was just a piece of ribbon or a jar of marmalade.

At this rate, she will never spend her monthly pin money or run up our accounts at the shops in Lambton!

Watching her with the tenants, his sister, Mrs Reynolds, and the shopkeepers made Darcy feel proud of his wife, and he shook his head at the thought that they might make a go of their marriage after all.

One afternoon in July, the new sisters were walking on a new path through the gardens. "Lizzy, you have seen most of the formal gardens. Would you like to walk out into the fields? My mother insisted on leaving much of the grounds in their natural state."

"Pray lead the way. I enjoy exploring the estate." As they walked, Elizabeth observed a lovely lattice and blue-stone structure in the distance. "Shall we walk to the folly?"

"Oh yes, let us go there! I used to play in it with my brother." As they walked, they heard a horseman coming from the opposite direction and watched as the rider stopped at the folly, dismounted, and sat on one of the benches. As soon as he was seated, he put his elbows on his knees and his face in his hands and seemed too distracted to notice the ladies approaching. Georgiana said excitedly, "It is Fitzwilliam. Shall we go meet him?"

Elizabeth stayed her friend's arm and led her away from their destination. "Your brother looks as if he has a problem he needs to solve. Let us give him his privacy and tell him this evening that we saw him this afternoon."

Later, while dressing for dinner, Elizabeth relived the scene at the folly. *Does my husband have as many concerns about our marriage as I do? Is that what is troubling him? Perhaps he is not as dismissive of me and our marriage as I once believed. Or is it simply a problem with the tenants? I pray he is thinking about making our marriage more than one in name only, for his sake and mine. My feelings for him are changing. He is such a loving brother, and he was kind and generous to everyone we met in Lambton.*

Later, when Darcy was seated with his wife and sister at the dinner table, Georgiana said, "Lizzy, would you like to go riding with me tomorrow morning after you meet with Mrs Reynolds? The weather is fine, and there are so many beautiful areas of the estate that are too far to reach on foot."

"I have not ridden very much, but I would be happy to accompany you after I have a few lessons and feel more comfortable in the saddle."

"Excellent! My brother is a wonderful teacher."

Knowing how much her husband disliked being near her, she tried to get them both out of what could only be an awkward situation. "Your brother is too busy running Pemberley to take time out to instruct me."

"Brother, do you think you could spare a little time to teach your wife to ride?"

"I would be happy to assist Elizabeth, but I fear I will be away from the estate again for much of the week. I will ask Jackson to help her. He is a very experienced teacher."

"Thank you." Elizabeth smiled at him. "Jackson instructing me will do very well."

"Brother, we saw you sitting in the folly today while we were out walking. You looked as if you had the weight of the world on your shoulders."

Elizabeth watched as Darcy's eyebrows came together, as if he feared what his sister would say next.

"You did not hear us coming near you, and Lizzy said you must have a problem you needed to solve and we should leave you alone."

Darcy hesitated and Elizabeth imagined that it was likely he had been thinking of their situation. The pause at the table grew long, and to end it, she asked, "Are you still worried about the trouble you had mentioned brewing between those two tenants?"

An unmistakable look of relief swept Darcy's countenance and, for once, he smiled at her. "Yes, Elizabeth. That is it precisely. I had just come from meeting with them, and we were no closer to a solution to their dispute than when I arrived. And while I much appreciate your consideration in leaving me alone, the truth is, I would have enjoyed some company."

Darcy's last words were uttered as he looked at his wife, and she felt her heart beating faster. Confusion made her cheeks grow pink, but before she could reply, Georgiana spoke up.

In a warm voice, she reminded her brother, "I told Lizzy that when I was a little girl we used to play there, and you would often read to me."

Darcy chuckled. "I remember you falling asleep on more than one occasion, and I had to carry you back to the house before you got too cold."

"Do not despise me now," said Georgiana, with an unusual note of mischief in her voice, "but I believe there might have been times when I woke and did not tell you, not wishing to be put down."

"Yes," said Darcy drily, "I confess that is not a surprise to me. I thought you might have been pretending at times, but it was a good test of my strength."

Elizabeth listened to her husband and sister speak so lovingly to each other. *My husband is a man capable of great kindness and affection. What can I do to have some of those feelings directed towards me? I believe we may slowly be growing closer, but I have no expectations until he decides how we are to proceed.*

As happened many evenings, Darcy and the ladies retired to the drawing room after dinner, where Georgiana would play the pianoforte, sometimes with Elizabeth's accompaniment. Tonight, however, Elizabeth chose to sit on the edge of a loveseat close to him. For a time, they sat in silence, merely enjoying the music together.

At length, Elizabeth spoke. "I received a letter from my father today."

"I hope all is well at Longbourn?"

"Thank you, yes," she replied. "He mentioned specifically that he believes any of the gossip about us from...from that day...has been laid to rest. The residents believe we married in haste so you could accompany me and the Gardiners on our journey north—territory with which you are very familiar."

"Thank you for letting me know. I am glad to hear it."

"There is also some much newer and more scandalous gossip keeping the residents of Meryton busy. People can always be depended upon to find something new to gossip about, particularly in a small town," she said lightly, and they shared a chuckle. "It appears a member of the local militia eloped with a young girl who recently inherited a great deal of money."

Darcy nodded his acknowledgement of the scandal that had replaced their own and hoped his wife would remain near his side. He wished to speak further so he could thank her for her timely intervention at dinner. It was pleasant, this little interlude of music and gentle conversation, and he cast about, trying to think of some other subject on which to converse.

Alas, too soon, she rose from her seat. Georgiana had begun a new, more complicated piece and seemed to be stumbling over it. "I believe I should go turn the pages for our sister."

He reached for her as she rose, but Elizabeth did not see his hand before he replaced it on his lap. "Georgiana can..." *Can what? Go hang? Turn her own pages or select a different piece?*

Elizabeth turned back and looked at him expectantly. Suddenly, everything he had wished to say seemed clumsy and awkward, so he said merely, "Of course. Georgiana will be glad of that, I am sure."

With a nod, she left him, taking a place beside his sister. Georgiana greeted her with an easy smile.

Darcy watched them fondly. He knew he must make some effort to speak to his wife. *Perhaps her riding lessons will be the place to start.*

The following afternoon, Darcy was on hand to begin the lessons. He watched from just outside the stables as Georgiana and Elizabeth walked down from the house. Taylor had altered one of Georgiana's riding outfits to fit Elizabeth perfectly.

The two ladies appeared surprised to see Darcy waiting for them, and before anyone could ask, he volunteered, "Bethel and I finished our tasks earlier than we expected. Jackson, help Mrs Darcy mount."

"Aye, sir. Madam, this mare is as gentle as a lamb, and she will help you feel safe in the saddle in no time."

Once Elizabeth was seated and the groom showed her how to hold the saddle horn, Georgiana mounted her own horse and walked beside her sister while her brother held the reins and slowly walked his wife around the paddock. "How do you feel, Lizzy?"

"Very well. Jackson was right about me feeling safe. Of course, we are just walking."

"That is precisely how I began," Georgiana assured her. "My brother and Jackson were wonderful teachers."

Darcy replied, "And now you are an accomplished horsewoman." He turned and spoke to Elizabeth, "Jackson knows better than to let anything happen that might lead to you being injured in any way."

Elizabeth looked at her husband and nodded, "I appreciate your concern for my wellbeing."

She paused then, and he wondered whether she wished to continue their conversation. For several awkward moments he cast about in his mind, seeking some other subject, but eventually he simply nodded. He then began the task of guiding her and her horse slowly around the paddock three or four more times until he finally turned back towards the stables.

When it was time for her to dismount, Darcy asked Jackson to help his wife. He had no desire to touch her in such an intimate way and give her the wrong idea about his feelings—feelings of which he was now entirely unsure. As they walked towards the house, Darcy noticed how well his wife looked in her riding habit but quickly put that thought out of his mind. The stirrings of attraction could not be given sway, not just yet—not when there was too much of her heart and mind which remained a mystery to him.

When they entered the manor, Elizabeth turned to him. "Thank you, sir. You helped me feel very comfortable in the saddle today."

"It was my pleasure, Elizabeth," Darcy replied before walking towards his study. Before reaching his destination, he turned and watched the ladies ascend the stairs. *She has been so kind to my sister and spends so much time with her at the pianoforte. I have often heard them laughing and singing together. At least my sister is happy with my choice of wife. I admired Elizabeth's courage today. She showed no fear doing something she had rarely done before.*

After dinner that evening, Georgiana asked Elizabeth to join her at the pianoforte. "We have been practising a duet, and I hope we are ready for you to hear it, Brother."

Darcy was delighted with the close relationship the two women had formed and thought again about how fetching his wife looked in her riding habit earlier that day, the dress tailored to hug her hips and accentuate her bosom. It was a dangerous line of contemplation, and he did what he could to push his mind away from such notions.

His sister began to play, and Elizabeth joined her before they both began to sing in harmony. Halfway through their song, Elizabeth hit a wrong note and they both laughed before resuming. Watching them, Darcy realised that another small piece of the cold stone in his heart had fallen away.

That night in bed, Darcy tossed and turned in his sleep. He kept thinking about his wife in her figure-hugging riding habit and his desire to have her in his arms. *Can I begin again with Elizabeth? Could we have a real marriage? She is intelligent, has lovely manners and a very caring nature. There is no pretension or artifice in her behaviour, unlike all the young belles of the* ton *I have met.*

He turned again, throwing aside some of his blankets. He felt, at once, far too warm. *I have no idea how we can start over, but I certainly must try.*

Georgiana and Elizabeth had become more than friends. Elizabeth felt—and she believed Georgiana did too—that they were truly sisters. One day, they were walking arm and arm in the garden, and the younger woman asked, "Lizzy, how did you know you loved my brother?"

How should I answer that question? Elizabeth knew that the girl could not be told the truth of things, but she did not want to lie outright. "Why do you ask?"

"I thought I was in love with someone last summer while I was in Ramsgate, but I soon found out that he did not care for me at all. All he wanted was my dowry of thirty-thousand pounds. I had known him since I was a child and thought I loved him and was prepared to elope with him."

"Elope? Georgiana, last summer you were but fifteen. Thank heaven it did not happen! What stopped you?"

"My brother paid me a surprise visit, and I told him everything because I wanted to share my good news with someone I love."

"I cannot think your brother received the news gladly."

"No, he was furious—with me and with my suitor. My brother told me I had been preyed upon by a habitual scoundrel and confronted the man the next day when he came to call on me. I overheard them arguing, and the reprobate called me terrible names and admitted he had never really cared for me—only my money."

Elizabeth reached for Georgiana's hand. "My dear girl, how you must have suffered. Are you happy now that your brother interrupted your plans?"

"Oh, yes. I know now that he prevented me from

making the biggest mistake of my life. When we were back in London, I was very unhappy and disappointed with myself to have been taken in by a scoundrel."

"Surely Mrs Annesley could not have been a party to this?"

"No, my companion at the time was an unreliable woman who it seemed was an associate of my suitor. Mrs Annesley was hired after we learnt the truth of her character." Georgiana turned to her then, earnestness and worry marking her countenance. "Pray do not mention to Fitzwilliam that you know what happened. It would only upset him to be reminded of that which is best forgotten."

"Of course, if you wish. You may depend upon my discretion," Elizabeth assured her with a smile.

The girl was relieved and offered Elizabeth's hand a squeeze as the two ladies resumed their stroll. "I am so happy my brother married you."

If only her brother felt that way. Thank heavens Fitzwilliam is a loving, caring guardian and saved his sister from ruin.

After eating breakfast one day in August, Darcy left for his study and Georgiana and Mrs Annesley left for her lessons. Elizabeth remained at the table to read the letters she had received that morning. One letter was from Jane, announcing her betrothal to Charles Bingley and expressing her wish that all the Darcys return to Longbourn for their nuptials, which would take place in September after the banns had been read.

"Oh yes," Elizabeth cried out, though she was alone in the breakfast parlour. "Yes, we simply must attend!" Excitedly, she walked to her husband's study, visions of Jane's happiness dancing in her mind, and entered after knocking.

"I have the most wonderful news. Mr Bingley has proposed to Jane! The wedding is in three weeks. When can we leave for Hertfordshire?"

Darcy looked up from the letter he had been writing. "I received a letter from Bingley stating the same thing. I am writing to him now with our regrets."

Elizabeth's delight plunged immediately into dismay. "Regrets? Why regrets?"

"Well, we cannot possibly make the journey."

She sank into a chair, feeling a lump in her throat, and resolved that she would not cry openly. A bit plaintively, she asked, "Do you not wish to attend your friend's wedding?"

"Elizabeth, it is a long journey, and you know I have been helping the cottagers every day with their crops and livestock before the harvest is ready. I fear it is simply not feasible right now to undertake such a trip. Perhaps we can visit the Bingleys and your family at a later date."

Elizabeth could not believe what she had just heard.

Bingley was her husband's closest friend, and he felt no need to attend his wedding. She looked at her husband as he resumed writing and walked out without saying anything more.

When his wife left the room, Darcy threw down his pen and ran his hand through his hair. *How can I be expected to travel for three days confined in a carriage, with a woman I feel I hardly know sometimes, even after living in the same house for months? Perhaps my feelings for her are beginning to change, but I cannot possibly behave as an affectionate husband in front of her family and friends. She must understand that I have no choice but to stay away from her until we know if we share any affectionate feelings for each other!*

Seven

September 1812
 Netherfield Park, Hertfordshire

Dear Lizzy,

Charles and I were disappointed not to have you and Mr Darcy at our wedding but understand how busy an estate owner is at this time of year. Except for not having you there, everything was just perfect. My dress, my hair, the flowers in the church, and the beautiful wedding breakfast in my new home were everything I have ever dreamt of. Charles is the most wonderful husband. He is so caring and solicitous of me that I fear he may not allow me to walk around by myself for worry I might trip on a rug! We enjoyed a wonderful wedding trip to Margate, and I enjoyed spending time at the seaside for the first time.

Papa told me he wrote to you about Mr Collins's visit to Longbourn, and since that time I can inform you of his marriage to Charlotte Lucas. Charlotte is the most amiable woman we know, and I am certain she will tolerate her obsequious husband well.

We are still enjoying the society of the militia that arrived in Meryton last autumn. Lydia, Kitty, and Mama remain over the moon with all the redcoats in town. They cannot decide which officer they are fonder of, the tall blond man or the dark-haired fellow who fills out his uniform very well. There was another officer of whom our sisters and mother were quite fond, but he eloped with Mary King when she inherited ten thousand pounds shortly after he appeared! Pray write as soon as you are able. I miss you terribly and hope you are happy. We plan to visit Pemberley next month on our way to Scarborough to meet my new relatives. Stay well, dear sister.

Love,
  Jane Bingley

When Elizabeth finished reading her sister's letter, she sighed with happiness at Jane's felicity in marriage. *Dearest Jane, if I could but know such contentment in mine.*

Darcy remembered what his wife had said about playing chess with her father, and one afternoon he invited her into his study for a game. She seemed, at first, surprised but readily agreed to the activity. After what he thought to have been an enjoyable hour, she left, and he thought back over what occurred.

Our conversation was limited to how we each learnt how to play the game. When our hands accidentally touched, I felt a jolt of feeling, but she quickly moved her hand away from mine and I attempted to continue playing without exposing my reaction to her touch. I cannot allow myself to have feelings for her! She does not seem to enjoy spending time with me. She always seems tense whenever I am near. Could it be because she is growing to like me more? I will not be made a fool by acting on my growing feelings before I know hers. We cannot go on like this—we must start talking to each other.

After dinner the following evening, once Georgiana excused herself from the drawing room claiming a desire to finish reading a novel, Darcy again suggested they play chess.

"I can move the set into the drawing room if you prefer to play in here."

"That is not necessary. Let us adjourn to your study."

Darcy seated Elizabeth before taking the chair opposite her. He watched as she set up her side of the board. The candlelight reflected off her lustrous dark hair, and when she looked up at him to start the game, he noticed the liveliness in her dark eyes. Darcy hardly knew what to say much of the time. While he had never been a man easy among the society of strangers, this was his wife. Somehow that left him feeling clumsier and more awkward than ever.

Elizabeth commented about one of his manoeuvres, he responded with a short answer—and that ended their conversation for the evening. When she admitted she was fatigued, he rose as she departed the room. He watched her walk and admired her light and pleasing figure and the way her hair bounced when she moved. He decided he would speak to her about their marriage the next time they were alone together; then he spent a restless night in bed trying to decide what to say.

Several days later, after tea, they were again playing chess while Georgiana played pianoforte for them. Darcy gathered his courage and asked, in a low voice, "Elizabeth?"

She raised her eyes from where she had been studying the chess board, arching one brow to urge him to continue. He did, albeit with some reluctance.

"It—it is strange, is it not, that we have been married many months, yet we have barely spoken more than a few words to each other."

"That is not true," she replied. "We talk all the time."

"I do not mean talk of inconsequential matters. I mean talk, really talk, about our marriage." He reached across the small table whereupon the chess board was arranged and touched her hand. "Perhaps if we talk about what our feelings are now, we can begin to rely on each other and grow to have some affection in our marriage."

Slowly, but with clear discomfort, Elizabeth tugged her hand away. "I am afraid I do not... That is to say, I do not think it would be advisable to have any such conversation."

"Not advisable?" He said it too loudly. Georgiana glanced over at them curiously, and he lowered his voice. "I believe it would, indeed, be advisable."

She pressed her lips together for a moment. "I am doing my best to serve as a good wife and mistress to your home and to find what happiness I can."

"A good wife?" he asked quickly. "You are my wife legally, but we both know in truth that there is much more to a true marriage than that."

"Truth?" She chuckled through a deep blush that was brought, no doubt, by his last words. "I do not think it wise to begin speaking the truth to one another. I have nothing to say and certainly no wish for a quarrel."

"There is nothing to say that should induce a quarrel."

"Is there not?" Her eyes flashed dangerously. "Very well then, I shall say this: I do not feel I can trust you."

"What?" His mouth fell agape a moment. "That is absurd. Whyever not?"

"On the day Georgiana arrived, I overheard your conversation with your cousin. We promised that we would keep the circumstances of our union to ourselves, yet you betrayed my trust and told Colonel Fitzwilliam everything within days of our agreement."

It could not be denied. He certainly had done that.

But she was not finished with him. "You have criticised, meanly, the behaviour of my mother and younger sisters, my lack of connexions, my non-existent dowry. You have faulted my father's indolence, and you have disdained my relatives in trade. I heard every word of what you said, the plain truth about how you really feel about me being your wife, with my own ears."

She rose, her hip knocking against the table and tipping the chess board onto the floor. The pieces flew and clattered all around her. She glanced down at them before turning and leaving the room.

Darcy exhaled forcefully. *She overheard me! I should have closed the door or kept the truth from Richard. Now what do I do? I made an overture, and she threw my betrayal in my face. Can I blame her? How would I feel if I heard* her *telling someone the truth of our marriage?*

"Brother?" Georgiana had paused in her playing and was looking at him with concern. "Is Elizabeth well? Shall I go after her?"

He shook his head. "Leave her be. I think she might have a megrim."

Elizabeth did not return to the house in time for dinner, and Georgiana spoke to Taylor and learnt that she had not gone to her bedchamber earlier but had left for a walk. "I am worried that she has been gone for so long," she said to Darcy. "Lizzy is not that familiar with the park."

"I will go look for her," he replied, "and if I cannot find her, we shall form a search party. Do not worry, little one. Your sister will be fine."

Darcy donned his greatcoat and hat and left the house. He remembered one of his wife's favourite walking paths, and a few minutes later, he found her sitting at the base of a large tree, clear evidence she had been crying on her face. She looked up at him as he approached. He counted it an auspicious sign that she did not flee from him.

"I hope you are not injured," he said gently, kneeling beside her.

She shook her head. "Forgive me, I know I have been gone too long."

"I cannot blame you for running out," he said. "Elizabeth, I pray you will forgive me. I am so sorry you overheard that conversation. Richard was here only a few days after our wedding, and I said those things before I knew anything about you. My feelings about your family are based solely on what I observed at the assembly in Meryton, and in hindsight, I recognise that the behaviour of some of my relations is no better."

"I do not defend the behaviour of my family," Elizabeth replied. "I dislike it as well sometimes, but they are, nevertheless, good people."

"I do not doubt it," he said. Then, wishing for no further secrets between them, he added, "I fear you over-heard me insulting you at the assembly as well, and I pray you believe me when I say I did not mean any of it. I should never have agreed to attend. I was angry at Bingley because I had just arrived from town that after-noon and I had not wanted to leave my sister." He sighed bitterly. "I shall tell you the reason for it someday, but not tonight. You are more than handsome enough to tempt me. I believe you are the most beautiful woman of my acquaintance."

Her quick glance showed a little doubt, but she did not pull away when he rose and helped her stand, nor did she remove his arm from her shoulders as he placed his greatcoat around her.

Georgiana had been pacing by the front door and was so relieved to see Elizabeth that she rushed to embrace her and inform her a warm bath awaited her. Before they climbed the stairs, Elizabeth turned and handed Darcy his coat. She nodded to him and turned back to her sister.

In bed that night, Elizabeth thought about Darcy's words. *He said I am the most beautiful woman of his acquain-*

tance, and he did not mean his insult at the dance. What am I to think now? Can I trust his words were sincere or was he only saying those things to get me back to the house? I am so unsure of everything in my life. If I reveal my changing feelings for my husband, will he respond in a similar way or try to shut me out as he has on so many other occasions?

The next morning, Elizabeth approached the doors of the breakfast room hesitantly. Her husband and Georgiana were busy eating and talking, and they both smiled at her entrance.

Georgiana looked at her earnestly. "How are you feeling this morning, Lizzy?"

"Much better, I thank you. A hot bath and a cup of tea worked wonders."

Darcy rose and asked, unexpectedly, "May I make you a plate?"

She offered a teasing smile. "That, sir, depends on how carefully you have been observing my eating habits."

"You prefer tea with milk and no sugar in the morning and either toast or a muffin with raspberry jam. And you often add some fresh fruit to your plate."

Elizabeth laughed. "Well done, sir! We might scandalise the servants—or my mother, should she see such a thing—but I shall thank you kindly if you prepare my breakfast."

Darcy smiled at his wife as she took a seat beside his sister.

He is being very attentive to me this morning. Did our

brief conversation last night force him to look at me differently? I never noticed him paying any attention to what I eat and drink, which is much better than the way he has ignored me these past months. Did I react too strongly when I overheard him telling his cousin the truth about our wedding?

Her husband, it seemed, wished to begin anew and though it was unsought, Elizabeth did appreciate it. Could she begin to trust him? Could she open her heart to him? She knew not but resolved she would not prejudice herself against him. She would greet him fairly and see where their new understanding took them.

It was not a week later when, after Elizabeth returned from an early morning walk, she heard several people speaking in the drawing room, a space that was rarely utilised during the day. Fearing she had forgotten some important visit, she hurried towards the room, utterly shocked by what—or whom—she found therein.

"Jane!" She clasped her hand to her mouth as her tears flowed freely. The sisters' embrace was long, and when they separated, Darcy offered his wife his handkerchief. Mr Bingley greeted his new sister, and everyone sat, Elizabeth still clutching her sister's hands tightly.

"Your husband planned everything," Jane told her.

"He had us stay at the inn in Lambton last night and sent a footman to let us know you were out of the house so we could surprise you when you returned from your walk."

"A wonderful surprise, indeed! I was so astonished to see you, I have been remiss in introducing you to my wonderful new sister, Georgiana."

"Charles already knows Miss Darcy well, and she and I had a wonderful talk while we were awaiting your arrival. I feel as if we are friends already."

Georgiana blushed at such warm kindliness. "Mrs Bingley, I would be happy to call you my friend, but please call me Georgiana. We are all family here."

"I would be happy for you to call me Jane."

"Now that we have settled that matter, would you like to have some breakfast, or would you prefer to refresh yourselves?"

Elizabeth smiled at her husband as the Bingleys explained that they had already eaten. A plan was formed for the day's amusements, and the Bingleys and Georgiana left to go prepare. She felt happier than she had in months and turned to her husband. "Thank you for this lovely surprise."

"The look on your face when you saw your sister is all the thanks I need." As she looked at Darcy, Elizabeth felt more content than she had in a long time.

That afternoon, Elizabeth and Georgiana showed Pemberley's beautiful gardens to Jane while Darcy and Bingley looked over some information necessary to running an estate. Bingley was eager to learn as much as possible before he purchased his own property and fulfil his father's wish of becoming a member of the landed gentry. The ladies were enjoying their stroll when Jane asked, "Lizzy, how do you spend your days? I am certain your husband occupies most of his time taking care of estate business. Pemberley has many attractions, but what else keeps you busy?"

"I walk early almost every morning, and after breakfast I meet with Mrs Reynolds to discuss the menus for the week and learn more about how the house operates and the cost of running such a large manor. I have been learning to ride, and Georgiana is kind enough to accompany me. We also play the pianoforte, but my skill is nothing to my sister's talent. Our library is filled with more books than anyone could read in a lifetime. Georgie and I often walk in the gardens before preparing for dinner, or I visit some of the tenants or the vicar in Kympton. I never realised that all the responsibilities of being the mistress of Pemberley would fill my days so completely."

"I should say so. It is lucky you have time to sleep!" The ladies smiled. "What about you, Georgiana?"

"I never rise as early as Lizzy, but I usually join her and my brother for breakfast. As you have already heard, I ride out with Lizzy most days and if she is busy, and if he is free, I ride with my brother. At least twice a day I practise my music and have lessons with...oh my goodness," Georgiana said suddenly. "I must leave you now. I promised Mrs Annesley I would join her in my sitting room. She received a shipment of new books and is eager for me to start learning more about English history. Lizzy, would you excuse me? It is such a beautiful day—I am so sorry to leave you so soon."

"We shall return in time to join you for tea."

"She is a dear girl," Jane said as the two ladies watched the other run off. "You are fortunate to have someone with whom you can enjoy spending time while Darcy is otherwise engaged. Your home is magnificent and so much grander than Charles led me to believe. How are you enjoying being the mistress of such an impressive home?"

"There is so much to tell you, and I am happy we are alone. There is a lovely folly near here and if we talk there, no one will overhear us."

Arm in arm the sisters walked together, and when they reached their destination, sat close beside each other on a bench. Jane gave Elizabeth a worried look.

"From your tone of voice, I can already sense that all is not well."

With a sigh, Elizabeth nodded. "We were total strangers when we married, and for some time, my husband did everything he could to maintain the distance between us. During our first weeks in Derbyshire, he rarely spoke to me and then only to answer a question. He has recently tried to talk a little more, and his arranging your surprise was completely out of character for him. He has never made any effort to get to know me or make my life more comfortable. Until Georgiana arrived, I had no one to talk to other than Mrs Reynolds and my maid."

"Oh Lizzy, surely after all these months you know him better now than you did before?"

"I know he does not beat his servants or kick his dogs, as I once feared. He is a loving brother and a kind and generous master, but in all the months we have been married, he has never touched me. A footman seats me at dinner, a stableman helps me mount my horse, and a coachman helps me in and out of the carriage."

"Obviously you have yet to..."

Elizabeth shook her head and looked at her feet. "Last week, we were playing chess and he tried to talk to me about the state of our marriage." Jane listened patiently as Elizabeth told her all that had transpired, leaving nothing out. She had hungered for this, a time to unburden herself to her dearest sister.

When Elizabeth finished, Jane looked pensive before she asked, "Have things improved since then?"

"They have," Elizabeth acknowledged. "It is all still

very new, but I am beginning to have more tender feelings for him. I admire his love for his sister and the way he looks after everyone he cares about. I have been visiting the tenants regularly, and every one of them has nothing but praise for him. He has apologised for what he said about me at the assembly and told me I was one of the handsomest women he knows. After the wedding, we resented each other so much and treated each other so unkindly, I cannot imagine how we can act any differently."

"Perhaps that is all he is capable of saying or doing right now," said Jane. "Charles told me Mr Darcy has always been a shy man and has never felt comfortable around people with whom he is not familiar. Hopefully, as time passes, you will grow closer and closer."

"I pray for that every day but do not have much hope of it happening." The sisters sat in silence until Elizabeth said, "It is starting to get late. Let us walk back now before Georgiana sends out a search party."

The sisters embraced and Jane kissed her sister's cheek. "All will be well. You are not made for ill humour. Have patience and be more receptive to him and hopefully he shall respond in kind."

"I will try, Jane. Oh, how I have longed for your wise counsel."

While their wives walked in the garden, Bingley and Darcy went over the newest books on crop rotation, animal husbandry, and other topics with which Bingley was unfamiliar. "Running an estate is a much harder job than I thought," he said with a grin. "The steward at Netherfield has taken care of everything in the short time I have held the lease there."

Darcy nodded. "As he should. You are only leasing it, after all. But you will wish to purchase something soon, I am sure, and then it will all be up to you."

"Yes, a purchase feels increasingly urgent these days."

"Oh?" Darcy asked.

"Since Jane and I returned from our wedding trip to Margate, Mrs Bennet has been a frequent visitor. Between us," Bingley said in a low voice, "a much too frequent visitor. Jane and I have discussed moving else-where, and we considered that buying an estate in Derbyshire might be the solution. You could continue to advise me, and Jane and Elizabeth could see each other often."

"I would be happy to help you in any way I am able," Darcy told him. "It would bring Elizabeth and me a great deal of pleasure to have you near."

"You and Mrs Darcy are...you are happy together? The marriage came about quickly, I know."

Darcy considered a few moments before replying. It was not in his nature to speak freely, but Bingley was family now; he was not a disinterested party. "When we arrived here, we treated each other as the complete strangers we were, and neither of us attempted to change that. Since my sister arrived, I have seen how charming and caring Elizabeth is. She has a playfulness about her that Georgiana enjoys and often tries to imitate. I have never seen my sister behave thus, and it warms my heart to see them together, laughing, singing, and playing the pianoforte."

"The only advice I will give you, my friend, is simple. Ask her about the things she likes and dislikes. Jane told me her sister enjoys nothing more than being out of doors and you must have realised by now she is clever and well-read. Mr Bennet educated her at home, it is true. Nonetheless," Bingley added with a shrug, "she knows as much as I ever learnt and, most likely, a great deal more."

"I shall try. I cannot promise you it will help, but I shall try."

"I can only pray that one day you will find the same joy with Elizabeth that I have with Jane."

The men shook hands and went to find their wives to join them for tea.

The day after the Bingleys departed to visit their Bingley relations in Scarborough, Darcy finished some correspondence at his desk and thought he might find Elizabeth walking in the gardens and have the opportunity to speak to her. As he walked towards the terrace doors, he could hear Georgiana practising in the music room and hoped that meant he might be alone with his wife.

As he looked about the garden, he spotted a flash of blue moving between some rose bushes, and when he got closer, he saw Elizabeth sniffing some flowers. He cleared his throat to make her aware of his presence, although she did look startled at the sight of him.

"I hope I did not frighten you," he said with a smile.

She offered a tentative smile in return. "I have been quite absorbed in inhaling the different scents."

"May I walk with you?" He stepped next to her and offered her his arm. She took it somewhat hesitantly, and it dawned on him that they had never before touched in this manner. It felt surprisingly natural.

"I am sure you must miss your sister."

"I do." Elizabeth sighed a little. "But I am very happy to see her joy and Bingley's as well. They are very well suited."

It could not have been a better opening for the subject

Darcy wished to speak of. "I feel likewise for Bingley. While he was here, we talked a great deal about his marriage and ours."

"Oh?"

"I explained to him how things stood between us." On her look, he added quickly, "He is family now, and he was there in Hertfordshire during the time when the events transpired."

"I see." Elizabeth nodded. "What did he suggest?"

Darcy turned to his wife and took both of her hands in his and placed them on his chest. Elizabeth raised her fine dark eyes to his and he fancied he could hear her heart thudding in her chest. An urge came upon him to kiss her but as soon as it did, he worried it would not be gladly received.

"Lizzy, Lizzy, there you are!"

The couple took several steps apart as Georgiana approached.

"The music is here! All the new music we ordered to play together just arrived, and I know you are anxious to look at it. There is still a little time before changing for dinner—" Georgiana stopped, gazing at them wide-eyed. "Oh dear, did I interrupt something important? We have waited so long for the package and when it arrived..."

Elizabeth shook her head. "I am just as excited as you are. Your brother and I were only talking and can continue our conversation later."

Darcy felt nothing but disappointed by the interruption. Charles had advised him to talk to Elizabeth and get to know her; but when they stood so close to each other, Darcy could only think about taking her into his arms. He had planned to gently kiss his wife and see how she responded. When he took her hands, she had not resisted. *Is it possible she has come to care for me as I have her? Somewhere along the way, I have fallen in love with my wife.*

Eight

October 1812

Phillip Bartlesbee, the sixth earl of Barton, sat across from his sister, Lady Henrietta, his eyes fixed on one of the more threadbare portions of the once-plush squabs. They had both dressed themselves in their finest, least tattered attire for the short trip from the family seat to Pemberley, and he could only hope it would be enough to impress Darcy and hide any hint of their increasingly precarious finances.

"Remember Hen, you must do everything in your formidable power to win Darcy over and get him to propose to you as quickly as possible. You are the only hope—"

"Yes, so you have told me at least a dozen times!"

"—of gaining the funds we need. Surely no loving husband could deny his wife the funds needed to save her family's estate."

Henrietta scowled at him. "Perhaps if you and Father had not squandered our wealth on gambling, drinking, and mistresses, there would be something left, and I should not have to sell myself to compensate for your errors."

"When a man becomes used to a certain lifestyle, it is nigh unto impossible to change it," Barton told her. "Be a good girl, now. He is a handsome man, so flirting with him should not be any great hardship."

Henrietta scoffed, not taking her eyes from the passing landscape. "Many before me have tried, Phillip. I do not know what arts and allurements you think I possess that those other ladies do not."

"Did not Marianna teach you some sort of...?" Barton did not wish to speak the words plainly. He had instructed his mistress to guide his sister, presuming to think that *she* would know what would work.

Henrietta did not answer, and it vexed him. Did she not realise how things stood? If the estate had no money, she had no dowry, and if she had no dowry, attracting any man would be nigh on impossible. But perhaps she was right. Perhaps the time for flirtations and courting was long past.

"Just do whatever is needed," he insisted. "If you cannot persuade him to believe himself in love with you, then we shall need to orchestrate some situation that depends upon his honour. As you know, his family and his reputation are everything to him. If necessary, we must create some scenario wherein he needs to spend some of his fortune to preserve his good name by marrying you or paying for our silence!"

Darcy was attending to some letters in his study when Mrs Reynolds entered, bearing the cards of Lord Barton and his sister Lady Henrietta. "Strange," he said, examining them. "I did not expect callers today. Was Mrs Darcy aware of this visit?"

"I think not, sir," the housekeeper replied, "unless she forgot, for she is not in the house at present. I asked them to wait for you in the yellow saloon."

Darcy barely suppressed a groan. Unexpected visitors and *he* would need to entertain them? Worse and worse. "If she is not returned in a quarter of an hour, send someone out for her. Have her join us immediately."

His own steps were excessively slow as he moved towards the room. He was acquaintances of long standing with Barton and knew him well enough to comprehend how badly he wished to see his sister settled. *There is a happy consequence of my marriage*, he thought. *No more matchmaking mothers or brothers.*

Barton and Lady Henrietta were seated when he entered, forcing himself to a welcome he did not feel. "I am surprised to see you," Darcy said to Barton. "I had not had word of your intention to call."

"We are on our way to a house party at Chesterfield," Barton told him. "Thought we might just stop for a bit."

This led to some conversation about mutual acquaintances and reminiscences, but throughout, Darcy became increasingly uneasy. There was an air of anxiety about the two that set him on edge. He found himself pacing, mentally hurrying his wife's return. After all, what good was there in a mistress of the house if all she did was wander the grounds?

A commotion in the hall interrupted his thoughts, but before he could react, one of the hounds burst in with Carter, the butler, hard on his heels. Behind them came the sound of Elizabeth's voice calling the dog to heel. Elizabeth herself soon followed, looking as dishevelled and muddy as she had that fateful day in the field in Hertfordshire.

For however shocked he was by her appearance, Lady Henrietta was ten-fold so. Looking distastefully at Elizabeth, she had the cheek to say—in a tone half-scolding and half-coquettish, "Really Mr Darcy, allowing a downstairs maid to enter your drawing room—and with a filthy dog no less! It is clear you need a woman to take this household in hand. This girl should be sent away immediately!"

Elizabeth was no less amused than she was embarrassed if the light in her eyes was any indication. Darcy walked towards her and stood right next to her, murmuring, "We have unexpected guests."

"Forgive me," she said quietly in reply. "Carter said I should come to you immediately; else I would have gone to change."

In his customary voice, Darcy said, "Elizabeth, may I present to you Lord Barton and his sister, Lady Henrietta Bartlesbee. Barton, Lady Henrietta, my wife, Mrs Elizabeth Darcy."

Without thinking, Lady Henrietta exclaimed, "Your wife?"

"We have been married these past few months." Darcy turned to his wife and smiled, "Elizabeth, I wished you to greet our guests before you change for dinner. Forgive me for hurrying you in from your walk."

"I thank you for your consideration, sir. Lord Barton, Lady Henrietta, I am happy to meet you both and welcome you to Pemberley." Elizabeth took some minutes then seeing to the guests' comfort. She ordered tea and bade them sit before saying, "Pray excuse me while I change for dinner. I hope you will stay with us?" Barton and Lady Henrietta both agreed with alacrity.

Darcy was delighted by the poise which Elizabeth demonstrated after being insulted by a stranger. She said just the right thing and appeared to be unaffected by Henrietta's disrespect, although Darcy knew she did not like being caught unprepared.

Barton had remained mostly silent throughout the brief time Elizabeth was with them, although his shock and dismay were plainly apparent. As soon as Elizabeth left the drawing room, however, he seemed to recover. "Darcy, what surprising news! I congratulate you, man. She is a beauty and very charming as well. I congratulate you and wish you very happy."

"Thank you, Barton, though I must confess I suspect she might be unhappy with my wish that she attend us without refreshing herself. My wife enjoys a long walk whenever the weather permits, but it does not mean that she would forsake propriety...nor that she would wish to be mistaken for a kitchen maid."

Darcy looked at Lady Henrietta after the last. The lady hesitated and did a poor job of hiding her disappointment when she said, "My apologies, sir. We had no way of knowing you were married. I congratulate you both. I would have remembered seeing the announcement of your wedding in the London newspapers."

"We wanted to keep the news of our marriage quiet so we could enjoy our privacy as long as possible. When we go to town in the spring, everyone will learn of my marriage and meet my wife."

"Of course," Lady Henrietta acknowledged, then rose. Elizabeth had directed Mrs Reynolds to prepare rooms for their guests' use and thus did the lady say, "If you excuse me, I will change for dinner."

Elizabeth called for her lady's maid as soon as she entered her chambers. "Taylor, we have unexpected guests and I look as if I was dragged behind the hay wagon. Please prepare a bath and help me decide which gown to wear tonight. I did not make a very good first impression, to say the least."

"'Tis a good thing Miss Georgiana gave you so many new gowns as a wedding present. One of those is sure to change their minds about what a fine lady you truly are."

"Taylor, you are a gift! Pray hurry, I cannot be late to join our guests in the drawing room."

Lord Barton was intrigued by the attractive young woman Darcy married. She was obviously not of the *ton*; he attended almost every fashionable gathering of the Season and had never seen her before. The women of Darcy's social circle would never be seen wearing the worn-out muddy gown in which she first appeared. There were too many untold details about their marriage. If he could learn the truth and it could be used to his financial advantage, all the better. If Darcy was sequestering his wife in Derbyshire, perhaps they were forced into marriage by a momentary indiscretion. All would be revealed by the arrival of the Darcy heir long before their first anniversary.

Well, if Hen cannot get to Darcy, Barton mused, *perhaps there is a second path to be explored with his wife.*

Lord Barton paid Elizabeth a great deal of attention at dinner that evening, complimenting her dress and hair and asking her if she would like more of one dish or another. Darcy watched him, pleased but also alarmed by Barton's seeming scrutiny.

Barton plied her with questions about their courtship and marriage. "Where did you say you were from, Mrs Darcy?"

With a gentle smile, Elizabeth replied, "My father's estate is near the market town of Meryton in Hertfordshire. Most have never heard of it who have never been there."

"Hertfordshire?" Lord Barton gave Darcy a look. "Darcy, I was not aware you had business in Hertfordshire."

"I do not," Darcy answered shortly.

"Mrs Darcy, how did you meet your husband?"

Darcy held his breath awaiting his wife's reply.

"My husband's friend, Mr Charles Bingley, leased an estate that is three miles from my family's estate. We were often together at assemblies and parties, and eventually we married."

Darcy was relieved by Elizabeth's answers. She only

told Barton a few bits of information without too many lies.

Lord Barton's interest did not wane once the meal had ended. After dinner, they all adjourned to the drawing room, and Lord Barton sat close beside Mrs Darcy as they listened to Lady Henrietta play the pianoforte and sing. Darcy watched closely, but Lord Barton did nothing untoward. Elizabeth seemed to be at ease with their guest, and thus he did not intervene.

Elizabeth found herself increasingly uneasy around Lord Barton. She knew not what to make of the man's friendliness. Was it genuine? She had to suppose that Darcy would have discouraged it, had he thought it inappropriate.

The following afternoon, Elizabeth and Georgiana were walking together in the garden when Elizabeth asked, "Are you much acquainted with Lord Barton and his sister, Georgiana?"

"I have met them in town when Lord Barton would call on my brother at our house there. He has always been perfectly amiable to me but..."

"Has he said or done something to upset you?"

"No, not that. It is the way he looks at me and at you as

well. He has an odd look on his face, as though he believes you want to kiss him. I cannot express myself clearly, but he makes me feel uncomfortable, and his sister is always fawning over my brother. I do not care for their company, and I wish they would leave as soon as possible."

"Lord Barton asks a great many questions and sits far too close to me whenever he has the opportunity. I confess he makes me uneasy too. I just could not understand why. Your feelings and mine are the same," Elizabeth sighed. "Well, I daresay I can only serve them well as their hostess and hope they move along quickly."

"Just be cautious around him. He and Lady Henrietta are two people I cannot trust."

"Thank you, my dear sister. I appreciate your advice."

It was only an hour later that Elizabeth was in the garden cutting some of the last blooms of the season, when she noticed Lady Henrietta walking towards her. She sighed. She was not looking forward to being alone with someone who insulted her at every opportunity. Lady Henrietta was dressed in a gown that seemed more appropriate at a dinner party than in a rose garden, but Elizabeth knew better than to compare her gowns to those of their unwanted house guest.

Lady Henrietta approached her hostess and, clearly

trying to appear friendly, asked, "May I join you, Mrs Darcy?"

"Of course." Elizabeth attempted to be civil and offered her guest a smile. "You find me cutting the last of our late summer flowers. I had hoped to get up enough for a few vases, but it seems the blooming season is well and truly done."

"I should have thought Pemberley would have someone to do such work."

"Of course," Elizabeth replied. "But I find it too enjoyable to be outside to relinquish the pleasure. This way, I can spend time in nature and not feel I am neglecting my house."

Lady Henrietta trailed behind Elizabeth, who could feel her guest's eyes on her as she went along the garden path performing an otherwise enjoyable activity. In an attempt to promote a discussion, Elizabeth asked, "Are you a lover of nature?"

Lady Henrietta took so long to reply Elizabeth began to think she might not. At length, she answered, "On the contrary. Other than riding occasionally, I prefer indoor activities. I suppose your fondness for the out of doors means you will miss being at Pemberley when you travel to town."

"I have lived in the country my entire life, so it is a far more familiar venue to me. Pemberley is the most beautiful place I have ever seen. London has many of its own attractions, I know, but I daresay I shall always prefer to stay here as much as possible."

Lady Henrietta appeared energised by her response. "Well, that is the case for many married couples," she said happily. "The wife remains in the country with the children while the husband takes care of his interests in town. You could always remain here and tend to your flowers and the tenants in your husband's absence."

Elizabeth knew not what to make of her enthusiasm and so only smiled and said, "Perhaps."

"To be sure! You seem to me to be a very independent, strong sort of woman and you should live where you feel happiest. Whatever Mr Darcy needs to take care of in London can be done without taking you away from this beautiful estate."

"That is true, but I am a married woman, and as such, I will do as Mr Darcy asks."

"And if he asks you to remain in Derbyshire?"

"As I have already stated, I shall reside wherever my husband wishes me. Now it is time to bring in the flowers and change my dress. Pray excuse me, Lady Henrietta."

As Elizabeth walked back towards the manor house, she could sense Lady Henrietta's eyes on her back, but she tried to put both of their guests out of her mind for as long as possible.

Georgiana, suffering a megrim, stayed in her rooms with Mrs Annesley later that afternoon, but her warning was not forgotten. Heeding her younger sister's words, Elizabeth was wary that evening with Lord Barton. His lordship seemed, however, perfectly amiable and did not behave in any way that was overly familiar or inappropriate.

After dinner, Lord Barton came to her as they walked towards the drawing room. "Mrs Darcy, Pemberley has so many extraordinary paintings in this room as well as in the gallery. There are so many lovely pieces, I would enjoy hearing about which ones you prefer."

Elizabeth glanced towards her husband, who, on seeing her look, said, "'Tis a fine idea, Mrs Darcy. Why do you not show his lordship the gallery for me?"

Was it a test of sorts? Elizabeth wondered. To her husband, however, she only smiled and nodded and then left the drawing room with his lordship.

Lord Barton and Elizabeth wandered through the gallery for some time, but as Elizabeth had only been in residence at Pemberley a short time, she had little knowledge to impart. Lord Barton seemed only faintly interested, giving the various statues and paintings cursory viewings. At length, Elizabeth began to wonder if he had detained her for a reason.

"I think we ought to return to Mr Darcy and Lady Henrietta," Elizabeth said finally. "No doubt they wonder what has become of us."

The pair was silent as they returned to the drawing

room. Just before they entered, Elizabeth paused, hearing Lady Henrietta speaking to her husband.

"...a country mouse! You cannot be happy with such a drab little creature, Darcy!"

Though she knew she ought not listen, she did, desperately trying to make out her husband's response. She could not, hearing only a low rumble.

"Exactly, right. Leave her here to play in the dirt as she wishes to, and you and I shall see what we can do to amuse ourselves in town, yes?"

In a rush, Elizabeth shoved open the door and entered, finding Lady Henrietta and her husband standing very close together by the mantel. Darcy took a step back when she entered, but Lady Henrietta did not, casting Elizabeth a meanly triumphant glance.

Elizabeth found herself preoccupied and wary for the rest of the night. She had not thought Lady Henrietta a friend, but did the woman have designs on her husband? Even knowing he was recently married?

She was roused from her musings when she heard her name. Evidently, a scheme was afoot for a ride out in the morning, and Lady Henrietta, still smirking, said, "Miss Darcy is unwell, but do say you will join us, Mrs Darcy?"

"My wife was never taught to ride in Hertfordshire and has only recently begun to improve her skills," Darcy said, speaking for her.

It stung, but Elizabeth managed to smile. "I thank you for the invitation, but unfortunately, I shall be much too occupied tomorrow. I hope you have fine weather and enjoy your ride." Thankfully, she could then slip back into her thoughts, watching as Darcy smiled and laughed with their guests.

I have no riding skills, play the pianoforte poorly, have no connexions to nobility nor anything else that would qualify me to be Mrs Darcy. No wonder he prefers the company of our guests to mine.

Lady Henrietta had made a slyly insulting comment about Elizabeth's gown earlier that evening, but her husband had said nothing. *Has he ever told me I look pretty? Evidently, he does not find me attractive despite what he told me the night he found me crying in the woods.*

As soon as it was possible, Elizabeth excused herself, saying she had a headache, and went to her bedchamber where she spent a long, lonely, and sometimes tearful night.

The two Bartons and Darcy went out riding the next morning. It was a pleasant time, as both were well seated, but Darcy wished his wife had accompanied them. *The terrain would have been too much for her*, he conceded in his thoughts. In any case, it proved best in the end. Barton had a matter pertaining to his estate to discuss with him that Darcy imagined would have been quite tedious for Elizabeth to hear.

Afterwards, as they were walking back towards the house, Darcy espied his wife sitting on a bench overlooking the lake and paused to watch her. Her feet were up, and she was twirling one of her curls as she read a book in a sunny spot.

An ideal place for a conversation about us, Darcy thought, wondering whether he should join her. *Not yet.* He decided he needed time to gather his thoughts before he spoke to her about their marriage. He had been pleased by the way she managed Barton's excess of attention, managing to divert him without offending him, and he thought she behaved admirably as hostess to the uninvited pair. *She does very well here.*

"Well, I daresay your wife was not too busy this morning after all," Lady Henrietta remarked, coming alongside him and taking his arm.

"She must have finished her tasks early," he replied, feeling a flush of consternation that had nothing to do with Lady Henrietta's charge.

Darcy excused himself from the other two as they entered the house. He walked to his study and gazed out the windows overlooking the garden. *When I saw her reading at the lake, something too powerful for words touched my heart. I love her. I have fallen in love with my wife. We married as complete strangers, but during our months at Pemberley, I have come to admire and adore her. Richard was right. She lights up every room she enters, and her laugh brings me deeper joy than I have ever known before.*

Mrs Reynolds came to Elizabeth as soon as she entered the house, telling her that the master was returned from his ride. She knew they had returned, of course. She had seen them coming across the lawn from the corner of her eye, laughing and chatting agreeably, Lady Henrietta looking particularly lovely in a riding habit that suited her figure admirably. At once she felt quite unequal to seeing him.

"Mr Darcy wishes to see you, ma'am," said the house-keeper, "but if I might...?"

"What is it, Mrs Reynolds?" she asked, feeling all the dreaded anticipation of her husband's satirical eye. Had she done something wrong to their guests? Did he intend to take her to task for some slight against Lady Henrietta? Or would he merely look at her, seeing all the ways in which she fell short when measured against a proper lady of the *ton*?

"I am terribly sorry to trouble you, but there is a problem in the kitchen between two of the kitchen maids. I have had no luck reasoning with them and, as mistress of the house, I hope you will be able to settle their dispute."

Elizabeth looked towards the hall that led to Darcy's study door. Surely whatever her husband wished to criticise her for—if even in his mind—could wait until later? With guilty relief, Elizabeth said, "Of course, I shall be happy to help if I can. Will you tell me what the trouble is about?" The ladies continued speaking as they walked towards the kitchen.

Nine

Darcy paced anxiously near the door in his study. He planned to take his wife gently by the hand and guide her to the loveseat where he hoped to speak to her about his changing feelings and his wish to begin again with their marriage.

When she did not arrive after half an hour, he asked a footman where Mrs Darcy was and learnt she had gone to the kitchen with Mrs Reynolds. *She would rather discuss dinner menus with the housekeeper than speak to her husband. I cannot blame her, I have yet to behave in a civilised fashion when we are alone. Maybe she needs more time, and I will wait until I believe she would be more amenable to being alone with me.*

Some minutes later, Darcy felt the thrum of excitement when he heard someone knock. He rose to open the door, imagining his wife on the other side.

"Oh. Lady Henrietta."

He knew he sounded disappointed but discerned it too late to alter it.

Clearly it did not signify to her. With a little laugh, she said, "Were you expecting someone else? Were you looking for Mrs Darcy?"

Darcy looked behind her and saw no one in the hall.

"Not at all," he said. He left the door open as he returned to the seat behind his desk. He gestured towards a chair at an appropriate distance from his own. "Is there something I can help you with, Lady Henrietta?"

"Actually, Mr Darcy, there is." Lady Henrietta's face creased with concern as she carefully closed the door. "You do not mind, do you? It is a matter of some delicacy, and, after all, you are a married man."

Darcy frowned. "Very well."

"I would never come to you with this problem if the situation had not become dire."

She was wholly earnest and seemed to have stopped the excess of arch teasing that she had plagued him with the evening prior. He had long known she had some design on him but could not comprehend why she might keep up with it now that he was married. In any case, it had ended, and for that he was glad.

"Pray continue, ma'am."

"You know my brother well enough to know that he has never been an active overseer of our properties. He told me that our profits have decreased to the extent that I believe our steward has been diverting off a great deal of money every year from the estate's coffers."

"This is a serious accusation, indeed," Darcy exclaimed. "Barton mentioned some confusion about the books, but he did not say that he suspected that. Has he confronted the man?"

"He made some gentle enquiry, but Mr Bradford denied any such thing and made some excuses about repairs and flooding. He was also my father's steward, so my brother's wont is to trust him. I tried having a peek at the books, myself but obviously I could make neither head nor tail of them." She gave a little shudder. "All those sums!"

Darcy frowned. "I see. That is very unfortunate. How can I help?"

"We have changed our plans and are returning home when we leave here. I wondered..." She bit her lip. Darcy could not discern whether it was a calculated attempt to look fearful or genuine alarm.

"You wondered what?"

"Would it be too much to ask whether you might travel with us? When we arrive, you could volunteer to help Barton check the estate books...or I could mention to him that you may be able to assist him. You know I would never ask you this unless it were urgent. I have no one else I trust! My dowry and the future of the estate that has been in our family for generations—" Lady Henrietta sniffed and wiped at a tear on her cheek. "You know it is only a day's drive from here. You could be back within a week."

Darcy cursed the timing of the request. To be away for a week now, with he and Elizabeth on the precipice of an improved understanding between them...but he knew they had no one else. Barton had no brother, no uncles, no one at all he could really trust. His father had been Darcy's father's intimate friend, and Darcy supposed he owed them something for that, if nothing else.

"I am honoured you would ask me," he said. "I cannot be away long, but I will come and do what I can to help."

"Sir, your friendship means more than I can tell you. I will leave you to your work and thank you." She left the room sniffling and went in search of her brother.

Darcy was still considering Barton's problems when, later that morning, Elizabeth knocked on her husband's study door. "You wished to see me?"

Now you decide you have time for me—two hours after I asked you to meet me? What should I do now? Elizabeth appeared wary, even mistrustful. He knew not why, but it was clear she was not of the mind or temper to hear what he had to say to her.

He smiled. "It is of no importance. You should know that I will be leaving with the Bartons tomorrow. They are old friends of the Darcy family, and they have asked me to help with some estate matters."

Was that a flicker of relief he saw across her face?

"Will you be gone long?"

"A week. Maybe more."

She nodded. "Very well. I will see you at dinner."

Lady Henrietta found her brother sitting alone in the library, staring out the window. "I am so glad I found you alone. I have wonderful news!"

With a wry smile, he asked, "Darcy has decided to buy you a house in town?"

"No, not that," she said with a smirk. "Although it may come in time. I convinced him that our estate is in financial trouble because the steward is stealing from us."

"You what?" Barton gave her a troubled look. "Bradford would never do that."

"Yes, I know," she retorted. "We have nothing but your gambling—"

"And your shopping!"

"—to blame for our woes. But Darcy does not know that. I told him you had already asked the steward about the money once and he denied it, and I said that you refuse to confront him again because he also served our father. Darcy has agreed to return to our estate with us to see if he can look over things and discern the source of the trouble."

"So, you will get him there and then—"

She gave a little wink. "Do as I must. A little indiscretion for a small settlement or, if I can manage more, I shall. I shall have to get him alone and see how agreeable he is to me once we are away from his country wife."

Barton chuckled, looking well pleased with her. "Well done, Hen. Let us plan to leave as soon as possible. I received a letter from my solicitor today, and it was not good news. Things are so bad I thought I might be forced to pretend I have some interest in the young Darcy girl to get my hands on her dowry."

"Well, you do need a wife, you know," Lady Henrietta mentioned.

Her brother stood and grimaced. "Not that badly I do not. Now excuse me. I have something I need to take care of."

Elizabeth was sitting alone in the garden with a little journal in her hand when Lord Barton appeared. "May I join you, Mrs Darcy?"

She offered a tight smile. "Pray have a seat, sir. You find me planning for next spring. I need to instruct the gardeners on bulbs and the like before the first frost."

He sat at a respectable distance from her on the garden bench. "I owe you an apology, Mrs Darcy."

"An apology?" She tilted her head, regarding him. He appeared to be sincere. "For what?"

"You are a lovely woman, and I confess that whenever I am near someone with your beauty I... Well, let me just say I know my behaviour was too forward at times. I sincerely meant no harm against you or my old friend here."

Elizabeth found herself feeling flustered by both his words and the compliments. "I... I thank you, sir. I assure you no offence is taken."

"Good, good," he said, then sat for some moments in silence with her. She suspected there was more he wished to say but knew not how to encourage him to say it. She had just resolved to rise and leave when he said, "Darcy has offered to perform something of a service for our family."

"Yes, I know." She gave him a sympathetic smile and added, "Do not fear, I know none of the particulars."

He waved that away. "I only hoped I might be equally helpful to you and him."

"How so?"

Looking at her very seriously, he said, "I hope you will forgive my candour, but so often I have looked at you and you seem...sad. I know you are far from your family and friends and thought it must surely be that which accounts for it.

"Yes," she said. "Yes, it is not easy being away from them."

"I would like to offer you my friendship, if you will. I know it is not the usual course of things, a man and a married woman being friends, but I think you may need someone here in Derbyshire."

"I regret that my emotions have been so obvious at times," Elizabeth said, wondering whether Darcy was embarrassed that his wife had been plainly melancholic before his friends. "I do miss everyone I was close to in Hertfordshire."

"You are much too lovely to ever be sad. You have the most extraordinary eyes. They sparkle when you smile, and I am a man who appreciates a few freckles on a lady's face."

Elizabeth chuckled. "I appreciate the compliment, but not everyone shares those feelings."

"Well, clearly your husband does. I know he has always admired them on my sister." Lord Barton grinned, looking very much at ease despite the blow he had just delivered.

"Has he?" she asked lightly. "Well, your sister is a very beautiful lady. I have no doubt she must have many suitors."

"She does, but none that she loved as she once loved Darcy. I am sure he has told you that they were quite close to an agreement when he travelled to Hertfordshire."

Elizabeth swallowed. "No, I did not know that." *Though surely it explains her bitterness towards me in my own home. No doubt she sees that it should rightfully have been hers.*

"None of that matters now," Lord Barton said as he rose to take his leave of her. "Darcy is a happily married man."

No, he is not. The words felt like a stab in Elizabeth's heart. *My husband was meant to marry Lady Henrietta. He would be happy if he were married to her and not to some country nobody. I should be glad he is leaving with his friends and will be happy.*

Darcy had not said how long he would be gone. Perhaps he intended to set up some sort of arrangement with Lady Henrietta, his true love. Would she be his mistress? Would she marry someone else and keep Darcy on the side?

She rubbed a hand over her forehead. *I was a fool to ever think this marriage could work.*

Elizabeth spent a sleepless night considering her best course of action, and as dawn arrived, she believed she knew precisely what she must do. Shortly after getting out of bed, she sat at the escritoire and began writing.

Mr Darcy,

I am writing to let you know that by the time you return from your trip, I will not be here. Since the start of our marriage, you have never looked at me except to find fault. I can easily see how unhappy you are, and I know I am the cause. You insulted me the first night you saw me although we had never been introduced or spoken to each other. I am leaving here so you will no longer have to look at me and be reminded of what you have regretted since that fateful day in April.

While walking around the park, I have seen several lovely cottages on the property. At first, I thought I might move into one of them, but being so near to the manor house would not serve any purpose. Georgiana has told me of a small estate you own in Scotland, and I plan to go there and decide what I wish to do next. I do not know how long I will be gone but have no plans to return to Pemberley.

Our marriage has never been consummated, and while I am in Scotland, you should apply for an annulment or divorce on those grounds or any other you choose, even desertion or infidelity. I hope you will allow me to use some of my marriage settlement to live on until I determine what I wish to do next.

If you prefer, I can sail to Canada and in a year or two you can have me pronounced dead and marry anyone you wish, and we can both put this unhappy union behind us. You can marry someone you love—someone from your own social circle whom you care for—and live a good life. You can be with Lady Henrietta or anyone else you prefer. Mr Collins told my father that your aunt Catherine was most displeased with our marriage. She said you were meant to marry your cousin Anne and soon, that may be possible. More than anything, I wish for you to be happy.

You were an honourable man to marry me—something neither of us wanted—and I thank you for saving my family from disgrace. I will tell Georgiana about my departure. I thank you for your understanding, and I hope you find the happiness you deserve.

God bless you,
   Elizabeth

When she finished her letter, Elizabeth placed it in her pocket and went downstairs. She found Georgiana and Darcy having breakfast.

"The Bartons have gone to finish preparing for the trip," Darcy informed her as she sat. Georgiana excused herself to go find Mrs Annesley. When the footman closed the door, Darcy dismissed the others.

"Elizabeth, I am glad we are finally alone. There are some things I would like to discuss... things I believe we need to say to one another."

Fear gripped her heart making her pulse race. Would he tell her he was going to apply for an annulment so he could be with Lady Henrietta? She found herself less prepared to hear him say so than she might have thought the night prior.

Her head was spinning, and she leapt up. "I...uh, no, I

mean, I forgot..." With panic beating in her chest, she blurted out, "Forgive me."

"Wait!" he cried out. "Elizabeth we are soon to depart—"

"Yes, uh, safe travels," she called behind her as she fled from him.

She nearly collided with Georgiana on the stair. "Lizzy," the girl gasped. "Lizzy, why are you weeping?"

Elizabeth had not known she was crying. Evidently, despite the things she had written to Darcy, a part of her had come to love him and dreaded the inevitable separation between them.

"May-may I talk to you? Privately? In your bedchamber?"

"Of course," Georgiana replied. The two ladies hurried into Georgiana's apartment, where she sat on the bed, looking at Elizabeth expectantly.

"Georgiana," Elizabeth paused, "it is not easy for me to say this, but I am leaving Pemberley."

"Leaving! Where are you going? To visit your family? When will you return?"

"I am going to Heatherwood and do not know when I will return." *I cannot tell her that she may never see me again. Saying it aloud would only break both our hearts.*

"Is my brother to go with you? Fitzwilliam will be back next week. He told me his travel plans when he said goodbye to me earlier this morning."

"No, when he returns, he will remain here with you."

Georgiana's eyes widened in shock. "Why? Why are you leaving us? I thought we had grown to be true sisters. How can you leave me?"

"You need not worry on that account. You will always be my sister," Elizabeth said as soothingly as she could manage. "I must go, but before I leave, I plan to spend every possible moment with you."

"I know you must have a good reason for leaving, but I shall miss you terribly every day you are away."

"I have written your brother a letter and I would appreciate you giving it to him when he returns." Reaching into her pocket, Elizabeth handed the girl her missive.

Georgiana gave it a dubious glance. "Of course. What-ever you wish."

Later that day, after Elizabeth learnt that her husband and their guests had departed, she and her maid were placing the last of her things in her trunk. They heard someone knock and Taylor answered the door. After a brief conversation, she returned carrying a letter. "For you, madam."

Elizabeth recognised her husband's lettering and assumed that although he did not know shc would no longer be at Pemberley, he wished to put into writing the terms of their separation and the arrangements he had made for her finances while he was away with the woman he loved.

There is time enough to read it on the road to Scotland. "Please place it in my travel case and I will read it on our journey."

When her trunk was packed, Elizabeth sat at her escritoire for the last time and began a letter to her sister.

Dearest Jane,
This is the last letter I will be writing to you from
Pemberley. Early tomorrow morning, I leave for
Heatherwood, the Darcy estate in Scotland. I have
asked Mr Darcy to seek an annulment or divorce.
As you know, our marriage has not been consum-
mated, and it should not be too difficult to obtain.

I am so desperately unhappy. You told me that I
should let my heart decide what I should do. I have
unexpectedly fallen in love with my husband, but he
despises everything about me and our marriage. I
have tried and tried to believe in a happier life, but
just looking at him shatters any dream I might have
of a brighter future. He stares at me with a scowl on

his face, looking to find fault in everything I do or say. He has never referred to Pemberley as our home and shortly after our wedding gave me 'permission' to read any books in the library as if I were only here temporarily. I have been treated as a guest in his home for the past seven months, and I know it would be best if I leave here as soon as possible.

I cannot blame him for resenting me for being forced into this situation. He only married me because he is an honourable man. He should have married someone of his own sphere, not the daughter of an indolent country squire. We recently had some visitors, old friends of my husband. Lord Barton told me that his sister, Lady Henrietta, and Darcy were close to being betrothed before Darcy travelled to Netherfield. He will be much happier with me gone, and my only wish is for him to find happiness. From what I have observed, he cannot be happy if he is married to me. I must work towards creating a future for myself—a future in which I can find some joy. I hope I can return to England in a year or two and start whatever life lies ahead of—

Her writing was interrupted when Georgiana knocked on her door. Elizabeth tried to shield her letter as her younger sister entered.

"I know you are leaving tomorrow and wondered if you will join me one last time at the pianoforte?"

Georgiana walked closer to the desk and glanced at the floor. To Elizabeth's horror she realised that the very words she had wished to hide had fallen, face up, in plain sight. Not wishing to draw attention to it, she did not bend to retrieve the letter and only hoped Georgiana had poorer eyesight than she.

"I will miss you while you are gone and hope to have one more happy memory of your time here."

"Of course, my dear. I was writing a letter to Jane but I shall finish it later. Give me a few minutes and I shall come directly."

Georgiana departed, seeming at ease. From her demeanour, Elizabeth presumed to think she had not been able to read the letter. She placed what she had written in the top drawer of her desk and left the room with cautious relief.

When Georgiana woke the next morning, she learnt that her sister had departed before dawn broke. She knew something was very wrong for her brother to travel in one direction while his wife was headed in the opposite. The little she had been able to read from the page on Elizabeth's floor confirmed that something dreadful was about to take place.

She had not been able to think of any just means to

stop her sister from going away. She had mentioned a few excuses the evening prior, but Elizabeth had brushed them all away with ease. She had even considered feigning illness when she woke to keep Elizabeth at Pemberley, but her sister had taken that possibility away by leaving so early.

Georgiana considered a moment, then sat down and wrote an express to her brother.

You are urgently needed at Pemberley. Pray return at once. It is a matter with Elizabeth.
GD

Ten

When they arrived at the Bartons' estate, an express from Georgiana was awaiting Darcy. Before he settled in his room, he read his sister's words and said, "Kenton, do not bother to unpack. There is an emergency at Pemberley, and I must return today."

"Yes, sir. Shall I inform Lord Barton?"

"No, thank you. I shall find him now and take care of it myself."

Barton was in his study and looked up when Darcy entered. "Are your accommodations not to your liking, Darcy? I did not think we would see each other until dinner."

"No, the rooms are lovely. Forgive me, but I must return to Pemberley straightaway. The express I received was from my sister, and she said it is urgent I return. I must make haste to try and be back today."

"Surely you can wait until tomorrow morning after you have eaten and rested," Barton protested. "You will never be back by dark."

"I feel I must try," Darcy insisted. "My sister would never have written unless it was absolutely necessary."

"Very well, then." Barton rose and shook his hand.

"Thank you. I regret I am not able to stay and help you, but I do wish for a speedy resolution to your problems."

The first two days of the journey to Scotland went smoothly. As Taylor helped Elizabeth prepare for bed in a modest coaching inn on the second night of their travels, she asked, "Have you read Mr Darcy's letter yet, ma'am?"

"No, not yet. Why do you ask?"

"When the footman gave it to me, he said Mr Darcy was very anxious for you to read it."

"It is in my valise. I will read it tonight if it makes you feel you have fulfilled your duty," Elizabeth said with a smile that hid her anxiety. "Good night, Taylor."

"Good night, Mrs Darcy."

Elizabeth reached into her bag and easily found the envelope. She sat on the bed and brought a candlestick close enough that she could read the only letter she would ever receive from her husband.

My dearest, loveliest Elizabeth,

Why am I able to write about my feelings with heart-felt honesty while I am unable to say these words aloud to you?

Elizabeth covered her mouth as her tears began to fall.

Our wedding was something that neither of us desired at the time, but for many months I have come to realise how truly happy I am that you are my wife. My feelings may be unexpected but are no less true for it.

From the first weeks living here together, I quickly came to appreciate your intelligence, wit, and kindness. I believe Georgiana fell in love with you before I did, but there it is. I love and adore you most ardently. You have captured me body and soul, and although it was unexpected, I will love none but you. The more time we spent together playing chess, reading in the music room while my sister practised, or listening to you and Georgie talking and laughing with each other or arguing about your favourite writers with Mrs Annesley, I fell more and more under the spell of the enchanting Elizabeth Darcy. I repeatedly heard reports of your kindness to our tenants and the neediest of our parish. Your jasmine fragrance has haunted my dreams and I have often tried to be near you just so I could enjoy your scent. I have watched you interact with Mrs Reynolds and many other members of the household with the same patience and kindness my dear mother always demonstrated.

I am so ashamed of how I have behaved. My parents raised me with good principles but left me to follow them in pride and conceit. I have always been retiring, but the way I treated you was monstrous. Please forgive a man who loves you with his heart and soul. I could often not take my eyes off your beauty, your tenderness to my sister, or so many of your other wonderful qualities.

I beg you to forgive my behaviour and allow us to start again. I plan to finish my business at Bartlesbee Manor quickly and return to you. I can never think of Pemberley as home without you beside me. You are everything I ever hoped for in a wife, and I was a fool not to tell you how my feelings for you changed months ago. You brighten my every day and inhabit my dreams every night. I could never be married to someone else. For me there will never be anyone but you. I wish to be married to you for the rest of my life, Elizabeth. I pray that you care for me, but I fear it is only my own desire. I still have hope that we can have a happy marriage if we speak to each other honestly. I need you in my life, my dearest wife. My only wish is that one day you will learn to care for me and grow to love me as I love you.

I am yours forever,
  Darcy

Elizabeth gasped and clutched the letter to her heart as her tears continued to flow freely. She read it once, twice, three times before she could truly comprehend and believe the sentiments contained within.

He loves me! I cannot believe it! He treated me with nothing but indifference and rarely said a kind word to me in all the months we lived under the same roof. What should I do now—continue to Scotland or return to Pemberley? I thought our marriage was over and that everything was settled between us. Now I am so confused!

Elizabeth's mind was full of conflicting thoughts, and she could not stop weeping. Taylor knocked softly on the door and entered. "I heard you crying, madam. Are you well? Is there anything I can get you?"

"No, I am sorry I disturbed your sleep. I thank you for encouraging me to read this letter." Elizabeth thought for a moment, then said, "I believe we will be returning to Pemberley in the morning."

Taylor looked relieved as she said, "Very well, madam. I will let the driver and coachmen know as soon as possible."

Alas the morning brought with it the news that the carriage had a broken wheel. Elizabeth had spent her night in a fever of anticipation, disbelief and many, many more re-readings of her letter.

"Mr Hubbard told me that the carriage should be fixed by later this morning," Taylor told her, no doubt wondering at her mistress's impatience.

With a sigh, Elizabeth said, "I suppose a few more hours will not make any difference. We can enjoy breakfast at our leisure and then begin our return."

A weary and dishevelled Darcy ran through the front door of Pemberley later that evening and found Georgiana pacing nearby. She heard her brother enter and rushed into his arms. "Thank you for coming so quickly."

"Are you well? How is Elizabeth? You said it was urgent I return."

"Elizabeth is not here, and she left you this note." Darcy had decided that as soon as he returned to Pemberley, he would have an honest talk with his wife and his sister.

"Gone? Gone where?"

"Heatherwood."

"Come with me." Darcy took his sister's hand and led her to his study where she sat and waited while he read Elizabeth's letter. When he finished reading, he looked at his sister, "Have you read this?"

"No, but I did find this unfinished letter in Lizzy's room." She handed him the pages she had folded and kept in her pocket. "I think you should also read this one."

As Darcy read what his wife had written, the only

words he read repeatedly were, "*I have fallen in love with my husband, but he despises everything about me and our marriage. He will be much happier with me gone, and my only wish is for him to find happiness.*"

His heart was pounding in his chest as he ran his hands through his hair. *She loves me! She loves me but thinks I despise her. I have been such a fool to keep my feelings to myself. She was so unhappy here. Could I have stopped her from leaving? What should I do now? My Elizabeth loves me!* Again, he focused on the missive in his hands but smiled when he looked at Georgiana.

"Brother, you *must* know why Lizzy went away and why she left without you?"

"Sweetling, please sit down and I will tell you everything. I should have explained it to you much sooner, but to start with, Elizabeth and I never fell in love in Hertfordshire."

Georgiana's brow wrinkled. "If you were not in love, then why were you married?"

Darcy told his sister the truth about the accident which led to his marriage. He spoke to her of his wrong impressions of his wife and then, most importantly, he told his sister how he had fallen in love with Elizabeth.

Georgiana considered it all, nodding when he finished. "I confess I had wondered why I rarely saw you alone together or why you never touched each other. You never escorted her to dinner or helped her into the carriage when we went to church. I thought you did not want to appear affectionate in front of me."

"I wrote her a letter before I left yesterday explaining how I felt and my hopes for our marriage. I asked whether we could start over when I returned."

"Are you certain she received it before she departed?"

"Before I left, a footman assured me that he would give it to Taylor, but I have to assume she did not read it. Surely, she would not have left if she had?" Darcy sighed, running his hand through his already tousled hair. "I love her so much, and now that she is gone, my heart feels like a cold stone. While she was here, I slowly began to have hope that we could have a real marriage but now—now she is on her way to Scotland. I know not what will become of us."

"You should follow her to Heatherwood," Georgiana suggested. "As quickly as possible, I might add. Go to her and tell her how you feel."

Darcy rose from his chair. "My sister has become the wise one in this family. I will leave tomorrow at first light to find my wife and bring her home." Darcy kissed his sister's head. "Thank you, little one. Rest assured, I will not return to Pemberley without Elizabeth beside me."

Eleven

The road north was still in relatively good condition. The first night, he slept at the inn he imagined Elizabeth might have stayed in, and he departed the inn early the following morning. After an hour or two on the road, Darcy's carriage stopped, and moments later the driver arrived at the door.

"What is the trouble, Paulson? We are in a hurry as you know."

"Yes, sir, but I believe Mrs Darcy's carriage is heading our way. I recognise Hubbard in the driver's seat."

"Signal him to stop at once."

Darcy alit from the carriage as the other vehicle stopped and Elizabeth's maid exited and began walking to meet him.

"Is Mrs Darcy in there?"

"Yes, sir."

Darcy tried to hide his smile, "I wish to speak to her alone. Please wait in my carriage until I determine our travel plans."

Elizabeth adjusted her pelisse as she waited for the maid to return. When the door opened, she was shocked to see her husband enter, close the door, and sit across from her. Neither of them knew what to say, and they looked into each other's eyes with uncertainty.

After a long moment, Darcy leant towards her and asked gently, "Were you coming home to me, Mrs Darcy?"

Her eyes swam with tears. "I read your letter last night, but I hardly know what to think. I was up all night trying to decide if I can believe you. You did not show me any affection in all the time we were together. You never expressed any feelings for me or your wishes for our marriage. I thought I was doing the best thing by leaving you to find happiness in your life, which is all I have ever wanted. I thought you were with the Bartlebees?"

"When we arrived at their estate, there was an express from Georgiana telling me to return home immediately, which I did as fast as I could."

"Were you sorry to leave Lady Henrietta?" she asked hesitantly.

"What? No, not a bit," he replied, sounding surprised. Before she could ask more, he added. "Elizabeth, do you want to believe that my love for you is true and ever-lasting?"

"I want to believe that more than anything I have ever wanted in my life."

"How can you believe I could ever be happy without you?" Darcy moved across the carriage and sat beside his wife. As he took her hand, he asked, "Why did you not read my letter before you left?"

Elizabeth shook her head. "I would have read it if I had known its contents. I expected your letter to be the terms of our separation and the financial settlement that would allow you to be with Lady Henrietta."

Darcy looked down at his boots and shook his head. "My love, we have not had a very good start to our marriage—so much stiff-necked pride on my part. But I can assure you that I have never had any tender feelings for Lady Henrietta."

He looked at their joined hands before meeting Elizabeth's intent gaze as she asked, "Is it too late? We are together now, but what lies ahead for us?"

"I have a confession to make," Darcy said quietly. "When you left without saying goodbye to Georgiana, she found your letter to Jane. She showed it to me, and when I read about your feelings for me, it felt as if all my dreams had come true."

Elizabeth nodded, remembering she had left the letter half finished. "Georgiana came in while I was writing it and asked me to spend some time with her. I suppose with all the last-minute packing, I forgot to retrieve the letter."

"When you told Jane you had fallen in love with me, I knew I had to go after you. When Paulson stopped the carriage and told me he saw your carriage heading south, my heart leapt in my chest. My only prayer was that you were coming home to me, and I felt so happy."

Darcy took a deep breath before continuing. "Now that we are face to face, there is so much I wish to say to you. I know when you asked what lies ahead for us, you did not mean an actual place, but what would you say to having a somewhat delayed wedding trip to Heatherwood?"

"I think a wedding trip to Scotland sounds lovely. We do have much to discuss, and I believe being alone together can help undo the damage we have inflicted on each other. But what about Georgiana? I hate to think of her alone for what could be many weeks."

"How could I not fall in love with you—someone who always worries about others before herself? Mrs Annesley is there, and my sister wishes more than anything to see us reconcile." Darcy opened the door and moved to step out. "I will inform the drivers of our plans and have word sent to Georgiana."

He took her hand and placed a lingering kiss on it before leaving the carriage.

How unexpected that a kiss on my gloved hand should send shivers down my spine! Perhaps because that was the first time my husband has ever shown me any affection, much less kissed me. If things go as I pray they will, I am certain I will have to get used to the more physical aspects of marriage. In fact, I am quite looking forward to it!

When Darcy returned, he sat beside his wife and closed the window curtains. "Kenton and Miss Taylor will follow us in the other carriage, and if we make good time on the road, we should be in Scotland in four or five days. Now, I have something important to ask you."

"Yes?" She gave him a little look. "Ask me anything you wish."

"Will you marry me?"

She laughed. "Marry you? My dear, we are already married."

"I know, but I never asked you for your hand. In April, we were forced into a betrothal in a muddy field with no questions asked. Today I ask you with a full heart, my dearest loveliest Elizabeth. Will you make me the happiest man in all of England and truly be my wife?"

"Does that also include Scotland?" she teased and then took his hands in hers. "Yes, sir, I will be your wife as I wish you to be my husband."

Darcy smiled at her response and kissed her gloved hand once again. "I brought something for you that I should have given you long ago." He took a gold ring covered in small precious stones from his pocket. "This was my mother's wedding ring, and I would be very happy to see it on your finger. May I?"

Darcy removed the glove on her left hand, slid the

thin gold band he had given her at their wedding off and placed the jewelled ring on her finger.

"I am delighted to have something that belonged to your mother."

"And my father's mother before that." Darcy took her hand, kissed the ring, and replaced her glove. "It is too cold to go without gloves. Allow me to cover you with another warm rug. I know there must be some under the seat." After he tucked the blanket around them both, she leant against him.

"You know, today is one of the few times you have touched me since our wedding."

Elizabeth saw shame cloud Darcy's expression.

"Will you ever be able to forgive me for being such a fool?" he said. "You once told me that you do not judge people by their wealth but on their character. I have demonstrated how poor my character was until I met you. I cannot think of any greater honour than to have you as my wife. There is no happy future without you by my side. I have not shown you that I am worthy of your love, but I will spend the rest of my life proving to you that I am. We will have ample time to discuss our short-comings, but I doubt either of us slept well last night. We can rest until we need to stop and change horses."

She rested her head on his shoulder and reached under the blanket to take his hand in hers.

My heart is beating so fast, and I am too excited to sleep! My husband came after me! He loves me, but I am not used to being near him.

Darcy spoke with his eyes closed. "I must confess that my heart is pounding in my chest. I fear I may not be able to sleep with my beautiful wife sitting beside me. I can smell your jasmine scent, and all I want to do is enjoy that fragrance for the rest of my life."

Elizabeth smiled and quickly fell into a restful sleep.

Darcy and Elizabeth sat next to each other the following day, talking and debating any manner of subjects, including a new bill that had been introduced in Parliament. "I suspect you are expressing opinions that are not truly how you feel," he said.

"My father loved to debate, and he and I would arbitrarily argue one side of an argument despite our true feelings. Did the belles of the *ton* express opinions of their own or just echo your thoughts so as to endear themselves to you?"

"Most often, the latter was the case," he said with a wry grin. "I love that you are so unlike them all. How can you have a discussion if one person has nothing original to say?"

He pressed her hand and continued. "I came to dread the entire Season. Spending more than one set on a dance floor with any one of the many 'eligible' ladies forced on me was a punishment. At least I know my wife will never run out of things to argue about, and I could not be happier about it. You are well read and kind and perceptive. Never pretend to be someone you think I want you to be. To quote my wife, 'all I want is for you to be happy'. I should have treated you better because you are my wife and I do not wish it to be any other way. After I began to admire you, I was too selfish and arrogant to reveal my feelings. Thus, I maintained my distance so as not to betray my changing emotions. I feared your rejection more than anything I could imagine. The last day you came to my study to play chess, I watched you between moves and forced myself to remain in my chair. "

"What would you have done if you had not controlled yourself?"

"I would have taken you in my arms and kissed you until you believed me when I told you the truth about my affection."

"Why did you not act on your feelings?"

"I feared you would slap my face and push me away."

Elizabeth shook her head, "How I wish you had. You read in my letter to Jane that I had already fallen in love with you, and although I would have been shocked by your behaviour, I would have welcomed any sign of affection from you. After all, we had already been married for months. I would either have returned your tenderness or turned away, but at least you would have done something to show me how you felt."

"I have been a complete fool and pray we can move past all these misunderstandings."

Elizabeth looked at him without replying and he enquired, "What is it?"

"Nothing is amiss. I was just thinking that we have already spoken more these past two days than in all the months I was at Pemberley. I would have liked having someone to talk to other than Georgiana. I would have been desperately alone without her and Mrs Annesley."

"As I said, I was a fool. Now I am a fool in love with his wife."

Twelve

A s the carriage ascended the hill leading to their destination, Elizabeth was happily surprised by the 'little' estate the Darcys owned in Scotland. The house was four times the size of Longbourn and had a rich red brick exterior. "Heatherwood is charming and so much bigger than I expected."

"Then it is better we are both here. The house would have been much too big for only you."

Before Elizabeth could respond, the front door of the house opened, and a middle-aged woman descended the steps. She looked startled as Darcy left the carriage first. She attempted to mask her surprise as she greeted him. "Mr Darcy, welcome to Heatherwood. We were not expecting you, sir."

"Mrs Marks, I am happy to see you. There has been a slight change of plans." Darcy helped Elizabeth down and smiled. "I would like you to meet my wife, Mrs Darcy."

Mrs Marks curtseyed to her new mistress. "Allow me to show you inside. Would you like to have something to eat or go to your rooms to refresh yourselves? Mr Darcy, I can have your chambers ready for you in a short time."

"Mrs Marks, I would love a cup of tea. Mr Darcy has

told me all about your special blend and after our journey, I could use some warming up."

"Of course. Right this way, madam."

Mrs Marks led her up the stairs and into the sitting room which adjoined their suites. While Elizabeth entered the room, Darcy bent his head and said quietly, "Mrs Marks, we are on our wedding trip, and as such we wish to be left alone as much as possible. When we need something, we shall ring, but other than that, we do not wish to be disturbed."

"I understand and will ensure your instructions are carried out."

Darcy entered the room and stood beside his wife, busy warming her hands by the fireplace. She looked up at him and said, "I knew it was cold here, but I underestimated how bone chilling it is, and it is only November."

As Elizabeth looked around at her surroundings, she added, "I will be very happy to spend my days in this cosy room with a warm fire and a stack of books. What more could I ask for?"

They exchanged a smile before she looked away and gestured at a door. "Where does that lead?"

"That, my dear, is the door to my bedchamber. I will lock it if you are worried I might take advantage of your proximity."

"I know you will adhere faithfully to our bargain until we are both ready to do otherwise."

Given the way that she blushed, Darcy thought it hopeful that such a time was not too far distant.

Their days were spent in quiet occupation—reading, walking, and a great deal of conversing between them. Several nights after their arrival, they sat together in the drawing room after dinner, and Darcy said, "I have been doing a great deal of thinking about us and have tried to determine why I behaved as I did."

"Have you come to any conclusions?"

"Yes, I believe so. Since I lost my father five years ago, I have been in charge of my own fate and, indeed, the fate of all those around me. I was spoilt and did not look kindly on anyone outside my family circle. I judged people on their wealth and social status compared to mine. I was given good principles that no longer matter to me. On the first day of our marriage, I looked at you in the carriage, feeling incredulous that you were my wife. You were a stranger to me, and I was furious with myself for being forced into a marriage which would have disappointed my parents if they were alive."

"My thoughts were quite similar, in some ways. Before the wedding, I told Jane the thing that bothered me most about being forced to marry was that I had no say in the decision that would change my life forever." Elizabeth had tears in her eyes as she added, "I am sorry you feel you have disappointed your parents by marrying me."

"I only mean to say that they would have wanted me to have a love match as they did. It was evident that was not the case for us. They may have been unhappy when we married, but once we began to care for one another, they would have loved you as I do."

Elizabeth blushed. "When did you know you loved me?"

He answered, "I cannot name a date or place. From your first day at Pemberley, I admired your warmth and kindness. But I think I knew I loved you the day you saw me at the folly. When you told Georgiana the story about a problem with the tenants to protect me, it touched my heart and showed me once again how caring you are."

Having decided to retire, they climbed the stairs arm in arm and for the first time, he gently held her face and briefly kissed her lips before they separated for the night. Elizabeth's first kiss felt like lightning had struck her. She took a small step back.

Darcy asked, "Are you well, my love?"

Smiling self-consciously, she said, "We have been married since April and this is the first time we have kissed in an affectionate way. Indeed, it is the first time I have been kissed by anyone other than my family."

"I hope it did not disappoint?"

Elizabeth blushed and looked at her feet before looking up at her husband as she said, "It did not. In fact, I hope perhaps we might do it again tomorrow."

"With pleasure, Mrs Darcy."

They walked out of doors as often as possible, and when the weather prevented it, they sat together by the fire in their sitting room. Some days they simply sat quietly while they read, and other days they laughed about their youthful escapades. They spoke about their childhoods and education. They compared their favourite activities: reading, theatre, opera, walking, riding, and their shared love of the out of doors.

Elizabeth spoke of her family, describing her parents and sisters in terms that showed her love of them even as she admitted to him some of their shortcomings. "Lydia is at the most trying age. She is too much a flirt and the most thoughtless of us all. Kitty follows where Lydia leads, and Mary, who considers herself quite pious, is always reading Fordyce. I believe my parents were in love when they wed, but over the years they became indifferent to each other. They are not affectionate people, and have little in common. He would rather read alone in his library and my mother prefers to be among friends and gossip. You can understand her eagerness to have us all married by the time she is left a widow. She is certain one of her daughters will take her in when the heir to Longbourn inherits the estate."

"My mother was the daughter of an earl, and as such, my grandfather told her in no uncertain terms that my father would never be considered a suitable husband for her despite his wealth, Pemberley, and his many other holdings."

"How did they marry if there was so much opposition?"

"My parents' love was deep and abiding, and in time my grandfather relented. I was born about two years after their wedding and when I was old enough to ask why my mother stopped spending time with me, I was told she was ill and could not leave her chambers. I later learnt that each time she was confined to her bed for weeks at a time, she had lost a baby. Each loss weakened her more, but she did not want me to be alone when she and my father were gone and did everything she could to give Georgiana life."

The most difficult days were spent discussing all the sadness and regret they both felt from the time of their wedding until they met on the road and decided to start fresh. There were recriminations and grief, but at length an understanding was reached between them.

"I promise you," Darcy assured, "I shall never again look at you with anything but all the love and admiration I feel in my heart."

"That will be a very nice change," Elizabeth teased. She waited a moment before she added, "Thank you for coming after me. When you entered my carriage, I was speechless. Knowing you cared enough about me to chase after me all the way to Scotland was everything I prayed for."

The days passed quickly as the Darcys spent almost every moment together, and every day their kissing became more and more passionate. At last came the night when proceeding further felt natural, even desirable.

Attired in a silky nightgown and matching robe, Elizabeth donned a second robe, a thick woollen one, and sat at her desk to write a short note.

> *My true love hath my heart and I have his,*
> *I hold his dear, and mine he cannot miss,*
> *His heart in me keeps me and him in one;*
> *I cherish his because in me it bides.*
> *My true love hath my heart and I have his.*

She knocked to get her husband's attention and pushed the paper under the door of his chambers. She quickly returned to her bedroom and hoped Darcy would soon arrive.

In his own bedchamber, Darcy heard a knock. No one entered when he replied to it. At length, he left the warmth of his bedclothes and went to the door, finding a folded bit of paper on the way. After reading it, Darcy quickly pulled on his breeches and crossed their sitting room to enter his wife's chambers for the first time. He found her standing in the middle of the room and held the page aloft for a moment.

"Mrs Darcy, I hope it was you who placed this poem under my door?"

"Yes, it was." She then untied her heavy robe and allowed it to fall to the floor. She was instantly chilled by the cold air, but the intensity of Darcy's gaze started a warm feeling in her belly. "I thought, perhaps, you might be willing to help me keep warm?"

His heart pounded as he went to her. "I will keep you warm tonight and every night for the rest of our lives." Taking her in his arms, he lifted her, placed her in the bed and then lay beside her. "I love you so much, but I must ask, what made you decide to ask me to come to you tonight?"

"I let my heart decide," she whispered as she turned into his arms.

Epilogue

After spending their winter at Heatherwood, Darcy was pleased to surprise his wife with a trip to see her family. As the date of their departure neared, they almost cancelled the journey. Elizabeth was alternately ill and exhausted for some weeks. Her suspicions were confirmed in March by a midwife who assured her she would soon feel more like herself. By April she did, and thus it was that May found them travelling to Longbourn.

The Bennets were delighted to see them and offer all the congratulations and felicitations that Elizabeth's state demanded. Bingley and Jane had their own happy news to share, and many an hour was devoted to telling each other all the little stories and reports of the time since last they met.

Now, on a sunny spring day, the grass was turning green, and the leaves on the trees were beginning to bud. Elizabeth and Darcy walked arm in arm in silence, her head leaning into her husband's arm. "Where would you like to go, my dear?"

"I want to see where we became betrothed last year," she said.

"Are you certain?"

"Yes, I need to be there to remember what happened and never think of it again."

Darcy took her gloved hand and kissed it. Again, they were quiet as they walked and were soon among the brown stalks of the tall grasses where they were found. They separated and each walked around the area where they first met.

"How are you feeling?" he asked. "There is a fallen tree over there. Let us sit for a moment."

She sat beside him, leaning into him and resting her hand on her lower abdomen. "I can hardly remember what I felt then. Everything has changed so much."

"For the better, I hope," he said.

"Fishing for compliments, Mr Darcy?" she teased. "Yes, very much so. I think back on that morning and how my life changed so drastically in a few minutes. How I hated you that day! When you said you would marry me if it was absolutely necessary, I thought I would faint! It was the worst day of my life, undoubtedly. I went out for my morning walk, and an hour later I was betrothed to a total stranger—a gentleman I had heard insult me the night before."

"I shall never forgive myself for speaking so."

"But it all led to this," she said, turning shining eyes towards him. "Every step, inauspicious as it might have seemed, has been a step on the path leading us here. I could never have imagined that our accident would lead to how full of love my heart feels now—but so it is."

"I believe we must agree to think of the past only if its remembrance gives us pleasure," he suggested.

"A very good philosophy indeed," she agreed happily.

He helped her stand and she embraced him. "Thank you for being the gentleman who saved this damsel in distress. If you had left me sitting in the mud, we would not know the happiness we have together."

"It was my pleasure, madam, and if you ever need saving in the future, you can count on me." They kissed tenderly and began their walk back to Longbourn.

ABOUT THE AUTHOR

Lily Bernard grew up in the Southwest and now resides in the land of sunshine and palm trees (with only an occasional hurricane). She fell in love with Jane Austen many years ago and a new world opened to her when she discovered Jane Austen variations. Lily is a retired speech pathologist who loves to spend time with her family and friends, travel, cook, and read, especially anything related to Jane Austen.

An Unexpected Love is Lily Bernard's seventh Pride and Prejudice Variation and she has several more works in progress!

facebook.com/lily.bernard.52643

ALSO BY LILY BERNARD

A Love to Remember

An Invisible Thread

At the Garden Gate

Mr Darcy's Destiny

New Beginnings

The Harvest Ball (New Beginnings Book 2)

A THANK YOU FROM THE AUTHOR AND PUBLISHER

The publisher and the author thank you for choosing *An Unexpected Love*. The favor of your rating or review would be most appreciated.

You are cordially invited to become a subscriber to the Quills & Quartos newsletter. Subscribers to the newsletter receive advance notice of sales, bonus content, and giveaways. You can join at www.QuillsandQuartos.com where you will also find excerpts from recent releases.